NAILED

Also by Amie Stuart

HANDS ON

On sale now from Aphrodisia

NAILED

AMIE STUART

A

APHRODISIA

KENSINGTON BOOKS

http://www.kensingtonbooks.com

KENSINGTON BOOKS are published by

Kensington Publishing Corp.
850 Third Avenue
New York, NY 10022

All Kensington Titles, Imprints, and Distributed Lines are available at special quantity discounts for bulk purchases for sales promotions, premiums, fund-raising, and educational or institutional use.

Special book excerpts or customized printings can also be created to fit specific needs. For details, write or phone the office of the Kensington special sales manager: Kensington Publishing Corp., 850 Third Avenue, New York, NY 10022, attn: Special Sales Department, Phone: 1-800-221-2647.

Aphrodisia and the A logo Reg. U.S. Pat & TM Off

ISBN-13: 978-0-7582-1893-3
ISBN-10: 0-7582-1893-1

First Trade Paperback Printing: June 2008

10 9 8 7 6 5 4 3 2 1

Printed in the United States of America

To the Chicas

ACKNOWLEDGMENTS

A huge thank-you to my critique partners, Raine Weaver, Denise McDonald, and Michelle Miles. Without you to kick me in the butt, keep me motivated, listen to me whine, and take me to the bar (Dennie!), I never would have finished this book. Rock on, ladies!

I also have to thank Kellie Hobi for the great title, which is where it all began; Tempest Knight for the information on Puerto Rico, which is where it all ended; and Bailey Stewart and Missy Shears for being my final set of eyes.

ACKNOWLEDGMENTS

1

Nothing, and I mean nothing, pissed me off more than having people stand around watching me work. And right now I had about a half dozen of them clustered around the pool's security gate. Dressed in bikinis, one-piece swimsuits, and cutoffs, they shuffled from foot to foot and chatted among themselves, praying I didn't ruin their day.

You couldn't blame them, really, for wanting a swim—not when it was 103 in the shade. But if they'd stop leaving their shit in the pool to get picked up by the filter or sucked up the drain, and stop burning up parts and . . . Sweat trickled down my cleavage. My head dipped under the weight of my ponytail, the aforementioned heat, and a healthy dose of frustration.

I sighed and wiped my forehead with the back of my hand, wishing *I* could go swimming today. August in Southwest Texas was the equivalent of a vacation in hell—in more ways than one. I'd about had it with doing apartment maintenance. Maybe it was time for me to move on, find something less taxing. Something cooler, like maybe being a supermodel.

I closed the cap on the poor drain thingy (technical lingo is *not* my forte) and crossed to the pump, switching it on. It slowly chugged to life, and I breathed a sigh of relief. I'd tried everything I could think of, and I didn't think the assembled crowd would be pleased if I had to take off for Cielo's one and only Internet café for more troubleshooting. Since coming to Cielo, everything I'd ever learned about fixing anything I'd found on the Internet.

I loaded up my tools and gave the assembled crowd a stern look while briefly ticking off each familiar face, then tossed Tara Woods a bikini top that looked suspiciously like the one she'd been wearing last week, except more mangled. "I'd really appreciate it if you'd keep your swimsuits out of the drains."

In addition to the swimming attire I'd finally dislodged, the pool was a particularly bilious shade of green that said too many carpet creepers had pissed in it. I didn't even bother smothering the bubble of glee as I cheerfully called out, "Pool's closed today, folks."

I'm sure in some former life I'd been a sadist, and in some future life, I'd pay for my enjoyment of their misery.

Scowls, grumbles, whines, and gasps of outrage were the response I got. *Please, people, if you want to use the pool, don't piss in it!*

"Thank Tara, everybody."

Tara smirked in return and walked away. The polka-dot bikini she was wearing barely held in her naughty bits. Of course, the only person complaining was Mrs. Hollis in 3-A. Guess she got tired of watching her thirteen-year-old wander around with a mini hard-on. He was in the laundry right this minute, washing his sheets. Yeah, I know . . . ew! Not something I wanted to spend too much time thinking about.

"Sen'rita." The sound of my assistant, Tony Ramirez's, voice got me moving. And for the record, he spoke English just fine; he just liked to keep me on my toes by playing the "dumb wetback"—his words, not mine. "The Johnsons need a new garbage disposal."

Toolbox in hand, I stepped through the metal gate that surrounded the pool and let it clang shut behind me. A new garbage disposal meant a half-day trip to Home Depot, which is why we normally tried to keep at least one around for emergencies, but we'd had a run on them lately. I didn't even want to know why. Regardless, I'd come to love Home Depot as much as I'd once loved Neiman's and Saks.

Okay, not totally, but life gives you lemons and you make Lemondrop shots.

The residents of Marquez Terrace Apartments were nothing to write home about, but then I had no home to write to anymore. No more Neiman's Christmas catalog, no more manicures, no more gourmet cooking classes, no more sister to go shopping with.

Guess that made us even.

One thing you had to understand about Cielo, Texas, and Southwest Texas in general was that if you weren't born here, you came here to get lost. This is where Tony Ramirez had probably come to get lost, where Tara and Jeanette and maybe even Old Homer had come to get lost.

And it's why I was here.

2

Wynn Collier pulled into Cielo, Texas, and eased down the main drag, taking note of various landmarks. Seventeen and a half months of his life, most of it spent on the road, retracing the footsteps of a woman who'd turned out to be more clever than he'd imagined, had brought him to this. He laughed softly to himself and turned down the sound of Nickelback coming from the SUV's speakers.

Despite its name, Cielo was a long way from heaven. Some might even say it was pretty close to hell, being miles from anywhere and surrounded by desert. Hell indeed—even the nearest Wally World was an hour away.

Police station—four cops and the sheriff. *Check.*

Volunteer fire department—with less than three thousand residents, anything that caught on fire would probably be an inferno by the time the troops were rallied.

His dark blue SUV slid past the café, three gas stations, an assortment of tourist traps disguised as antique stores, and stores selling Western/Texasy paraphernalia that women like his mother went nuts for. Not that the town had a bustling tourist trade; it was too far off the beaten path. Which explained why his quarry had chosen it.

Nearly eighteen months of hunting down Julie Burt had brought him here, to the end of nowhere.

Most of the time, Wynn's job involved going after bad men, the dregs of society. Drug dealers, thieves, murderers, con men. People smart enough to know that when they played with fire, they risked getting burned. Not ordinary, middle-class people who believed crap like the Sopranos was purely a result of someone's overactive imagination.

He didn't kill people, much to his father's disgust, but he knew how to get information out of them. That was his job.

Hunting down people like Julie Burt and her family had left a really bad taste in his mouth. Unfortunately, he hadn't been in a position to tell his dad no. But he'd follow his dad's instructions to the letter, find Julie Burt, and discover where her sister and brother-in-law were, get the information they had so Dad could get it back to the client.

Nothing more. Nothing less.

At Main and Elm, he took a left and proceeded to drive the entire town, familiarizing himself with the streets and landmarks, like the poor dinky elementary school and, just a few blocks over, the equally small library next to a nondescript city hall. The houses ranged from a few single- and double-wide trailers to World War II bungalows with deep porches to modern ranch houses. Nothing fancy, though, and nothing too new.

Cielo wasn't that sort of town.

The world seemed to have passed Cielo, Texas, by. Everywhere he looked, everything seemed dead, lifeless, and flat but for the mountains shimmering in the distance. Just the type of town no self-respecting, normal person would live in; just the type of place someone could easily hide in.

But, oh, what a long way the slippery Ms. Burt had fallen.

From designer suits, a Lexus, and selling commercial real estate to . . . a town practically burned to a charred husk by the searing heat.

He pulled his ten-year-old Blazer, which was guaranteed to not stand out, onto the shoulder of the road with a crunch of tires on gravel. It came to a rest underneath a giant scrub oak. The oversized branches didn't even move but did provide some shade.

The beige brick apartment building across the road practically faded into the landscape. The grass around the sign was the greenest thing he'd seen since he'd left downtown. These were the best Cielo had to offer. Hell, they were *all* Cielo had to offer. He'd laugh if he didn't have so much riding on this job.

He saw neither hide nor hair of any humans as he pulled his digital camera from the bag on the seat beside him. He snapped pics of the four dust-covered vehicles in the parking lot then made the short drive back to his motel.

At the Shadyside, Wynn stepped inside his darkened room, quickly closing himself off from the stifling heat, and dropped a two-inch-thick file containing everything on Julie and her family onto the bed. He scrubbed a hand across his head and caught his reflection in the dresser's mirror. He looked tired. A lot more tired and older than he really was. And if his mother could see him, she'd say he needed a haircut.

He spent the rest of the afternoon going over his notes, and thanks to his wireless card, shot the photos he'd taken to his mother. He knew better than to hope that a motel in the middle of nowhere would have Internet, let alone wireless, so he'd brought his own. Judging from his room's gold and avocado furnishings and the nightmare-inducing bedspread covering the queen-sized bed, he was lucky they even had HBO.

When he'd done all he could, he stretched out on the bed

with the file. Julie Burt, formerly a successful commercial realtor in Scottsdale, had up and disappeared within hours of her sister's apparent death. He'd been tapped for the job when the first two "companies" had failed to produce Julie or her sister, Karen Lyons.

In the ensuing months, he'd come to admire Julie's resiliency and her ability to stay a free woman, to stay under the radar. But the clock was ticking, and the client was turning the screws, wanting the job finished in two weeks. He didn't know why, and he didn't care. It wasn't Wynn's place to ask why. It was his place to do his job and, if possible, get out undetected. Life was less painful that way.

He dozed off, bothered by dark dreams of Julie and buzzards, until the phone ringing woke him up. Outside the tightly closed curtains, a bit of red-tinged light seeped in, alerting him to the coming night.

"Does an eighty-four Corolla look as bad as it sounds?" his mother asked, referring to one of the license-plate photos he'd sent her.

"It's a nice shade of rust, with a little sky blue for accent." Smiling, he sat up and took a swig from the bottle of water on the nightstand. It was warm but wet, which was all that mattered. "Any of those cars belong to Julie?"

"You didn't think she'd have one registered under her real name." Her chuckle was a rusty but comforting sound.

"Of course not, but everyone slips up eventually."

"True. I gather you haven't found Ms. Burt yet, then?"

"Not yet." He sighed, thinking of the job ahead.

"You'll be fine, dear. I have *complete* confidence in you," she reassured him. They could have been talking about a job promotion he was up for, not the latest assignment his father had thrown his way.

Hunting down Julie Burt wasn't much more than table

scraps in the scheme of things but (a) it kept his father off his back, and (b) it gave Wynn a chance to redeem himself after botching that last job. He honestly hadn't meant to blow off three of Doug Garrofolo's toes. Matter of fact, he normally didn't even work with guns, preferring more subtle means of persuasion. But his oldest brother, John, who had come along to supervise, had insisted Wynn carry.

The Colliers were men of few words who let their guns speak for them, and as such, they had fine reputations as hit men.

Then there was him, Wynn, the bane of his gun-toting father's existence. To be honest, he preferred to let his intimidating 6'5" height and muscular body (and well-known name) speak for him. Wynn enjoyed the challenge of getting what he wanted or needed from people by using his wits and words, not violence—unless it was absolutely necessary. When faced with one of his ham-sized fists, most people didn't put up much of a fuss, and if they did, well, it didn't take much arm twisting to convince them to give up the goods.

He might be the shame of the Collier clan, but he had the respect of those who preferred a more subtle, less-violent information-collection method. And he was damned good at what he did.

"Wynnie . . . are you still there? Do you have everything you need?"

"Yes, ma'am."

"What about a sweater? I heard it gets cool there in the evenings. That mountain air, you know."

"I'm fine, Mom. I promise." He scribbled notes while she rattled off the names and background information on the other car owners, gave her his love, and rang off.

It was dark outside; time to get moving.

3

The sun had finally set when I stepped outside dressed in battered Sketchers, cutoff sweats, and a tank top with no bra. The barest hint of a breeze lifted damp pieces of my freshly washed hair and struggled to blow away the day's heat. A near impossible battle.

From the open window, Clyde meowed his protest of my desertion. You'd think he'd have gotten used to it after a year. Every night after dark, I walked the complex, greeting the occasional swimmers, and the few people who sat outside drinking beer, and I listened . . . and watched. My guilty secret. I refused to name it, to call it what it was.

I'm sure people who smoked crack said the same thing, but the first time had been an accident. Eight months ago, I'd been walking the back of the complex, working off nervous energy, the edge that had ridden my back ever since I first ran. The fear, the paranoia it had taken me nearly two years to shake, and even now, another year after, I still couldn't completely let my guard down. *Where was I? Oh, yeah . . . walking.* I'd rounded the corner and spotted a couple in a parked car. It had been fall, still warm in the evenings, but they'd had the windows up, and a hint of fog obstructed my view. The movement of the car had said it all.

Inside, a topless woman had been riding Dinky Smith like she was going for the Triple Crown, her ginormous breasts bouncing happily.

I'd been helpless to move, a prisoner of my body, of my need, of my own frustrations and loneliness. There I stood after two years of celibacy, watching Dinky Smith have something I couldn't . . . sex, intimacy, affection.

Call it whatever you'd like, the weight and depth of it all had almost killed me that night.

That had been a Wednesday. I'd gone out on Friday, to Busters, and picked up a tourist, thinking if I fucked him, I'd never spy on Dinky again.

I was wrong.

I found myself lying in wait for him (he apparently *liked* having sex in cars). Then I found myself following him, watching him. He'd never caught on—I'd been real careful. And, you know, he wasn't the brightest lightbulb in the package. The legality, or illegality, of what I was doing was irrelevant when held up next to the Big Picture. *Trust me on this.*

After a while, the weather turned colder, and I'd gotten bored with Dinky. I found myself drawn to casually peeking in kitchen windows. They were huge, forty-eight inches wide and sixty inches off the ground. I'm 5'5" and that made us a perfect match.

Then came the bedroom windows, listening, straining my ears in the dark to hear couples fucking and fighting.

Anyway, tonight was Thursday, and Darcy McKnight's boyfriend was coming over. Normally boyfriends were no big deal, but Darcy was cheating on her husband, Chris, and for the record, she wasn't the only cheater at Marquez Terrace.

Chris was a long-haul trucker who came in on Sunday and left first thing Wednesday morning. Darcy wasn't dumb enough to have her boyfriend come on Wednesday; she waited a day. No one ever told on her; no one dared. Guess you could say we had our own don't ask/don't tell policy.

And besides, Chris was a giant who'd probably kill the bearer of bad news, and Darcy's peccadilloes weren't worth dying for, but Brad was.

He came by around 9:00 every night, slipped in her front door when most people were ending their day, and, well, Darcy had a bad habit of leaving the kitchen curtains open, and the window too.

My stomach was a tangle of excited nerves as I spotted Brad slipping into Darcy's apartment, the open door briefly spilling lamplight on the sidewalk. I walked the upper floors so as not to raise suspicion. Then I took the stairs, greeting Old Homer, who sat in a lawn chair he kept just outside his front door.

"Gonna be a hot one tonight."

"And sticky too," I said, pulling my tank top away from my body and fanning myself for effect.

I walked the front of the U-shaped complex, then circled around the back, taking my time. I knew already that Brad's truck was parked at the convenience store half a block down, and the owner was a friend of his.

The front of the complex faced the street with the complex's sign and the pool blocking the view of just about anyone from the road. An old SUV sat on the gravel shoulder across the street. Probably overheated, which was a common occurrence around here in the summer.

Down the side of the building I went, rubber soles silent on the hard-packed earth. I stopped at the back corner of the building to catch my breath and listen. All I could hear was the sound of the occasional cricket, the buzz of a mosquito that I

swatted away, and someone's radio playing a Mexican station—
all of that over the excited beating of my heart. God help me, I
hoped Darcy never got caught.

One last glance over my shoulder, and I turned the corner,
keeping a casual, steady pace. Three windows down, I stopped,
my back pressed to the brick wall, and listened.

An immediate, "Oh, Brad!" prevented me from peeking in
the kitchen window. It sounded like they were at the kitchen
sink, though I knew they weren't. It sounded like he was spank-
ing her with the spatula again.

For sure.

And trust me, Darcy didn't mind. I sent up a little prayer of
thanks as my curiosity got the better of me. I turned my head,
raising up on my toes to find her bent over the little wooden
kitchen table she'd refinished last summer, her bare-naked ass
in the air, shining a sassy red.

Brad wore a faded black T-shirt stretched tight across his
broad shoulders and nothing else. I could see straight through
to the living room where his jeans and boots and Darcy's clothes
lay scattered about. His muscular legs weren't very tanned. Brad
wasn't the kind of man to lie around in the sun. His forearms
were tanned, though, and his hands were huge and probably
callused. His ass was lily white, two perfect, muscular half-
moons, and his dick was beautiful. Hard and thick and strong,
jutting out at an angle from a dark nest of pubic hair.

Beautiful enough to make me take my truck in to his garage
every three thousand miles for an oil change just so I could
watch him work and fantasize about his cock.

I'd tested the waters, flirting a bit to see what he'd do, and
he'd responded, but I always seemed to chicken out when it
came to asking him to dinner. Call it self-preservation, but I'd
reluctantly decided that fucking tourists was a safer bet for the
time being.

Once Darcy's ass was nice and red, he fucked her from behind. I stood there growing hotter by the minute, my pussy throbbing as I watched his cock disappear between the cheeks of her ass. She squealed and chattered like a fucking angry squirrel.

"Brad, fuck! You're so big!"

"You like that?" he asked, mashing his hand into her hair and holding her head against the table. "Huh, you little slut?"

"Oh yes!"

"Better than your fucking husband?" he panted.

"God, yes! I love your cock. Fuck me . . . fuck me more!"

"Little dirty girl."

He'd call her a whore and tell her what a bad girl she was every single damn time, but I never got tired of hearing it. My hand slid up my thigh, into the leg of my shorts to massage my pussy lips, but that wasn't enough. I slid my middle finger deeper, circling my clit faster and faster, my lower lip caught between my teeth, my shoulder pressed into the brick wall. My toes curled. I closed my eyes and stroked myself, listening, imagining it was me.

Until a nonsexual sound penetrated my lust-filled brain. I squeezed my eyes tightly shut a moment in frustration before opening them again and licking my lips and slipping my hand out of my shorts.

I knew better than to act suspiciously. Instead, I moved slowly, turning toward the parking lot and scanning for movement. I didn't see anyone, but I'll be damned if it hadn't sounded like a cough. Maybe it had come from an upstairs apartment but I wasn't about to risk it. I backtracked to the corner of the building, detoured out into the middle of the parking lot, and continued my walk, slowly scanning the gloomy perimeter for signs of life. Nothing, no one, nowhere.

Playtime was over.

That feeling of unease that had bothered me the last couple of weeks, that same one that had finally subsided over the last couple of years, had grown worse lately, leading me to believe it was almost time for Bonnie James to disappear and for someone else to take her place.

4

Wynn ducked down behind the car, his night-vision goggles gripped in one hand.

A Peeping Tom. He'd nearly gotten busted by a damned Peeping Tom. He knew she'd been watching someone having sex. Even from this distance they'd been hard to ignore, their moans drifting out the open window and across the parking lot. And if the peeper's body language was any indication, she'd really been enjoying herself.

From what he could tell, the peeper was pretty, petite, compact. Her dark brown hair had been gathered up in a sloppy ponytail, but it would probably reach the middle of her back. She had a curvy ass, full hips, and high breasts.

She wasn't his quarry, but she'd proved to be an interesting diversion.

He stayed put as she doubled back and passed no more than six or seven feet from where he was hidden between a pickup and a beat-up, ancient SUV, before disappearing from view. He eased to his feet, adjusting his erection and waiting until she disappeared around the far side of the building. He waited a few minutes longer to make sure she didn't return, then slipped from his hiding place and crossed the parking lot to the window she'd been looking in.

Inside, the couple was on the couch, the man's legs splayed out wide, the woman on top of him, her hips wiggling, her curly blond hair bouncing in time with her movements.

Peeping Toms and perverts. Grinning, he silently stepped away and circled back around to the front, his pace slow so he could memorize what was where and give his blood time to cool.

He imagined Julie Burt in one of those apartments, sleeping peacefully, lulled into a false sense of security, assured that no one knew where she was, fully unaware that trouble was about to arrive on her doorstep.

Wynn still hadn't ID'd his quarry, and the clock was ticking. The following morning, he took a few passes through town, stopped to eat at Cherrie's Diner, and chatted up the waitress. Spending the day sitting outside the apartments was a big no. The last thing he needed was some small-town, tin-star-toting deputy getting a bead on him, so he'd bided his time.

If there was one thing Wynn had learned from tracking people down, it was that bars and greasy spoons were hubs of activity and gossip. He'd struck out at Cherrie's but hoped to have better luck at Busters, Cielo's only bar.

This late on a Friday night, the place was packed, the parking lot full of dusty pickups and an assortment of cars, the mouthwatering smell of the barbecue pit outside permeating everything. Inside the corrugated tin building, there was one bartender, two pool tables, and a jukebox with a dance floor no bigger than a postage stamp.

He nodded at the swarthy Mexican at a crowded table who

caught his eye as he took a seat at the bar. A woman resembling Wynn's peeper sat with him.

"What'll it be?" the bartender asked. He was tall, gray-headed, and just starting to run to fat, a slight potbelly visible under his white T-shirt, which was covered with an ugly plaid short-sleeved shirt—the kind you'd get at Wal-Mart.

"Scotch and water." Smiling, Wynn pulled some bills from his wallet and set them on the bar top.

He sipped his drink while watching the group behind him through the mirror. The cute Peeping Tom—what did you call a female peeper?—was behind him, dressed in snug-fitting Levi's and a snug-fitting tank top. She sat sipping at a beer and trading rapid, off-colored yet good-natured insults with the Mexican who'd eyed Wynn earlier.

The bar was filled with an odd mix of what looked like tourists, people dressed like him in khakis and expensive but casual polo shirts, and the locals, many of the men dressed not much different from the bartender, many of the women dressed a lot like the hottie behind him. Locals seemed to outnumber the tourists by three to one.

He saw more than his fair share of short, chubby women, even a few blondes, but none of them were Julie Burt.

Wynn couldn't afford to be distracted. His career—no, his life—depended on it, but oh what a distraction his little voyeur would be. If his father knew what he was thinking . . . He pushed that thought away as the waitress appeared at his elbow, slid another drink at him, and nodded toward the pretty brunette. She raised her bottle in a silent toast and joined him.

She was tanned and fit and healthy, not the fitness-club, tanning-bed-healthy either, but the kind brought on from hard work and semigood living. "Where you from?" Emerald-green eyes twinkling, she leaned into him, an inviting smile on her face.

Wynn liked a take-charge kind of woman, and he had a feeling she didn't deal in bullshit. "Oklahoma City."

"You're a long way from Oklahoma City."

"Vacation."

Her laughter drew a censorious stare from the bartender. *Interesting.* "This ain't no vacation, sugarpie. *Cozumel* is a vacation. *Italy* is a vacation. *This* ain't no vacation."

She was right.

He laughed, too, as they clinked bottle to glass. "Maybe I just needed to get away."

"You picked the place for it." She leaned into him again, a gleam of understanding in her eyes. "What's your name?"

"Wynn," he said before he could stop himself. Something in her eyes had prevented him from lying as he normally would have. As he *should* have. But he had the distinct feeling she could smell a lie a mile away.

"Like, *I always win*?" She grinned at him, her eyes crinkling at the corners. Her face had character. She had to be at least thirty, maybe a few years older than he'd originally thought.

"W-Y-N-N, Wynn," he corrected, leaning into her. She smelled like sunshine, vanilla, and lemons. "And you?"

"Bonnie . . . Bonnie James."

"Like Jesse and Frank?" he asked, filing it away.

"Exactly."

"So what are you here to steal?"

"Maybe I just want to borrow." A smile curved her pretty lips, but it didn't quite seem to reach her eyes. She was a bit calculating. And she'd take what she wanted. He could respect that. He didn't hold with that bullshit about women being sluts and men being studs anyway.

Whatever she wanted to borrow, he was more than willing to loan it as long as he got something in return. In Bonnie James's knowing gaze, he forgot all about Julie Burt, about his father, and about the ticking clock and his brothers who would come hurtling through town in no time at all, leaving death, destruction, and missing relatives in their wake.

He'd earned a night off, hadn't he? The tightness in his Dockers and Bonnie James's cleavage said he damned well had. Besides, Bonnie might come in handy—at least in terms of information-gathering.

His gut tightening in anticipation, Wynn leaned in closer until only a few inches separated their lips. "What would you like to borrow?"

"You." She laughed, leaning away and tossing her hair over her shoulder, teasing. Sending out all the right signals.

They sat there a bit longer, finishing off their drinks, engaging in chitchat, sizing each other up, each of them silently debating whether to invest in (at least) a few hours of hot, sweaty stress relief.

"You from around here?"

"Sure." Her eyes slid away, focusing on the mirror over the bar.

He followed her gaze but didn't see anything worth noticing. She was a liar. That made them even, since he was too. Even that didn't diminish his desire for her.

She fingered her cleavage, caressing the edges of her tank top in order to draw his eyes downward. He'd be less than a man if he resisted, even if a small part of his brain knew he was being seduced. He couldn't even blame it on the booze, not after only a couple of drinks, when she slipped off her stool and smiled at him, and he followed as if there were some invisible tether holding them together.

Outside, she pressed him against the side of his Blazer, her hand sliding down to stroke him through his jeans, while her tongue slipped past his lips, teasing and tangling with his, warming his blood in ways whiskey couldn't.

"Your place," she breathed.

* * *

She teased him all the way to the motel, nibbling at his neck and rubbing his cock through his jeans, ensuring he was embarrassingly hard when they stopped for the six-pack of beer she'd asked for. He'd nearly run a red light *and* a stop sign as she'd dug into his jeans, stroking his erection all the way from the convenience store to the motel.

He couldn't even think straight by the time they stumbled into his room.

"Condoms?" Bonnie dropped her keys and a tiny purse on the rickety motel table and kicked off her shoes.

He laughed, feeling slightly embarrassed, struggling to recover quickly. "I hadn't thought this would be that sort of vacation."

She laughed, too, a throaty, suggestive sound that teased his ears, and reached into her purse. "Don't worry," she said, holding up a string of three connected wrappers. "I'm always prepared."

They didn't waste any time or words, hastily stripping each other naked, then giggling as they fumbled with the condom. She wriggled against him, her button-hard nipples pressed against his chest, her skin hot underneath his as his fingers slipped between the swollen lips of her pussy. Her cunt was hot, tight, and hungry, grasping at him, wanting more. Bonnie was all business as she flipped over and pushed her ass in the air. She tucked a pillow under her cheek, sighing in obvious contentment.

Wynn found himself struggling to ignore his conscience and the itchy white sheets that smelled slightly of bleach. He pushed it all aside, forcing himself to ignore the distractions as he parted her cheeks and slid into her pussy.

Bonnie's eyes fluttered closed, and a smile tickled her lips as his fingers stroked her clit. Her hips moved with his, their pace increasing enough to make the bedsprings squeak underneath them. Neither of them was in the mood for anything that might be mistaken for love play as they used each other, the squeaking and their own harsh breathing the only sounds in the room until they collapsed in a sweaty satisfied heap.

Afterward, they lay in bed talking and sharing a cigarette. Sex was the only time Wynn smoked.

"Why in the hell would you pick a dead-end place like Cielo for a vacation?" She rolled on her side to face him, passing him the cigarette.

"Why would you pick a dead-end place like Cielo to live?" he countered, unwilling to talk about himself any more than necessary.

Bad enough she was in his hotel room.

The open, relaxed expression on her face immediately disappeared. She rolled over and climbed from the bed, getting them both a beer from the bucket of ice on the dresser. "How do you know I wasn't born here?"

"A good guess?" He tucked a few pillows behind his head, enjoying the sight of her naked going *and* coming as he accepted the can she handed him. He popped the top with practiced ease. "What about that guy at the bar? How do you know him?"

He sounded jealous, even though he hadn't meant to. It was a good cover, though, so he went with it.

Shrugging, she sipped at her beer, her mind apparently a million miles away as she rejoined him in the bed. "He's . . . like family. Married, got a kid; the usual shit."

"How do you know him?" So sue him for fishing; it was part of his job.

"I'm his boss," she said with a wry laugh.

"So, he works under you?" With a chuckle, Wynn rolled over and nuzzled one boob, pulling her pert nipple into his mouth.

"We've never"—she grinned, shrugging away—"I don't fool with the locals."

Interesting choice of words. It was the little things that got people in trouble, little things they rarely even realized they'd let slip. "Guess that explains how I got so lucky. What do you do?" He nuzzled her cleavage. "What keeps you here?"

"I work maintenance at the complex, and I stay here because I like it."

Could have fooled him. Even though he knew the answer, he had to ask the next logical question. "What complex?"

"There's only one, honey."

"Bet that keeps you busy." Though obviously not busy enough, if she had time to peek in people's windows.

"Not so much. There's only twenty-four units, and we're never full."

"How'd you fall into apartment maintenance?" He'd have to stop soon; this wasn't exactly postcoital chitchat.

"I tripped."

Evasive. She was being evasive. He sipped his beer thoughtfully, his eyes skimming the length of her. Not one scar marred her naked body, but there was the faintest hint of stretch marks on her belly, and he wondered if she had a kid somewhere. Was she running from an ex? He couldn't imagine any man getting the best of her, but there was no telling what she'd once been, what had driven her to become what she was.

She snuggled closer, her fingers trailing up the back of his thigh, registering a light electrical shock in the vicinity of his balls.

He rolled away, setting his beer on the nightstand to buy himself a little time before they ended up in round two, and then asleep, and he ended up with no more information out of her. She stroked his hip, her lips warm and wet on his back.

Fuck it. He rolled back over and covered her mouth with his.

* * *

24

The sound of the shower running woke Wynn, and the previous night came back in a flash that left him wishing he was in the shower with Bonnie. Especially when his cell phone started chirping with that special little ring that told him it was his father. If he didn't answer, the old man would just call back. And keep calling until he did answer. So much for shower sex.

Grimacing, he rolled over, grabbed the phone, and flipped it open. "Yes, sir."

"What's your status?"

Whatever happened to hello? Wynn knew the old man would be sitting in his mother's sunny yellow kitchen while she cooked up bacon and French toast—her Saturday ritual—while he sipped coffee and read the paper.

"Great," he lied, praying Bonnie stayed in the shower just a few minutes longer. "Everything's going great."

"Good—"

"Listen, Dad, are you sure Karen and Kevin Lyons are alive?" Lyons was Julie's sister's married name.

"As sure as I know that if you don't get their whereabouts from Julie Burt inside of the next two weeks, I'm sending your brother Will in. Wynn, I've told you, I have people counting on me to deliver! And if *you* don't deliver, *I* can't deliver. Don't fuck this up, son, 'cause there's no room for error *this time.*"

5

"I need to get going." I slid my damp legs into last night's clothes, enjoying every ounce of postcoital glow.

I watched Wynn hop from the bed, enjoying the sight of him naked, wishing we hadn't used up all the condoms last night. He was fit and tan, the hair on his chest darker than the short sandy hair on his head. And tall, very tall, with the equipment to match.

"Ahem."

"Sorry." I flashed him an apologetic smile. I could definitely use one for the road. But my pager was probably full of messages from tenants who had clogged drains or toilets, or they'd broken the pool again, or JoJo had found a trench for me to dig. "I've got to get home and feed Clyde."

"Clyde?" A wide-eyed Wynn froze in the middle of slipping on a fresh pair of jeans.

"Yeah, Clyde. He just turned four, and he gets really pissy when I leave him alone all night. He's kinda clingy." I'd said it so many times to so many other men, I didn't even laugh anymore. Like I'd leave a human child alone. *Puh-leeze.*

Wynn nodded but didn't say a word, just slowly slid into a pair of worn Levi's and a dark blue polo shirt.

"Will I see you again?" he asked once we were on the road.

"I doubt it. I've got a pretty busy week, and I'm on call next weekend. Things can get crazy." *How long could he be staying in Cielo anyway?* No one but an idiot like me, or someone born here, stayed here.

And to be honest, I wasn't super keen on seeing Wynn again. Despite his hotness quotient, something about the previous night's twenty-question routine made my Spidey senses tingle.

Not good.

You could never be too careful. After I'd gotten the hell out of Scottsdale, I'd watched every conspiracy movie I could get my hands on, including *all* the mob ones, and let me tell you, those guys didn't mess around. I wasn't one-hundred percent certain what had happened to my sister, Karen, but I knew I didn't want to end up like her.

Dead.

I spent the rest of Saturday schlepping around the apartment, milking my postsex mellowness for all it was worth, doing laundry and ignoring Clyde to the best of my abilities.

He wasn't even mine but Karen's. When he was little, he was cute, all gray with white socks, a white throat, and little white marks around huge eyes. Then he grew up, and those pretty amber eyes of his took a decidedly nasty turn.

They were evil. Like he was plotting just when he should kill me and where he'd start eating once I was dead.

It wasn't that I hated Clyde, per se, but that he was so damned *damned*! I'd finally decided that cats were like kids— cute when they're little but hard to predict which ones'll stay cute and which ones'll go all sociopathic on your ass. Think *The Omen* with fur and you had Clyde.

I'd get rid of him, but like I mentioned, he was my sister's, and in the very last conversation we ever had, she made me promise to protect Her Baby Clyde—*and who the hell names a cat Clyde anyway?*—with my life.

Call it survivor's guilt or whatever you want, Clyde was the king of the beasts, and I was his (sort of) dutiful (incredibly reluctant) slave.

Sunday was spent at the Internet café, discreetly researching out-of-the-way places I could get lost in. The more I thought about it, though, the better Canada sounded. Except for the cold.

I had money and a backup ID squirreled away, but payday was this Friday, and since I had no idea how long it would take me to find steady work, I figured a few more days couldn't hurt.

Monday I was up early, picking up trash and cutting the grass before it got too hot. On the way back to the storage shed with the edger, I noticed what looked like Wynn's Blazer in the visitor's parking lot.

Most of the residents stuck to parking in the back. I didn't believe in coincidences, but it looked like the one that had been parked across the street the other night—it looked like Wynn's. The thought pulled me up short. SUVs were a dime a dozen out here. It could mean something or nothing at all, but the desire to flee grew stronger.

Frowning, I wiped at my damp forehead with my arm and kept walking, but at a much slower pace, my eyes scanning the complex. I didn't see him lurking anywhere around, but the thought of imminent danger made me pick up the pace, replacing the edger and circling the complex as quickly as possible.

No Wynn. Anywhere.

My terror grew, the hair on the back of my neck prickling as I pictured him sneaking up behind me, a dangerous-looking pistol, complete with silencer, clutched in his very capable hand. A glance over my shoulder assured me my imagination was working lots of overtime.

From the pool came the sound of splashing. Jeanette Porter and her two little ones were out, determined to take advantage of the cool water before it got any hotter and the pool got too rowdy for the smaller kids. I waved at her while my eyes scanned the front of the complex again.

I couldn't put my finger on it, but up on the second floor, things didn't look right. And JoJo, the manager, hadn't stopped me once this morning when normally she was a total pain in my ass.

I skirted the pool as quickly as I could, picturing her fat ass laid out behind her desk, blood pooling around her body. Yeah, JoJo and I weren't exactly friends, and she wasn't exactly fat, just a dim-witted twat who'd gotten the job because she was engaged to the building's owner.

From JoJo's office came the sound of the Rolling Stones whining about satisfaction. *Get in line.*

Dismissing thoughts of JoJo, I slipped up the stairs as silently as possible. The leaves of the shrubs around the pool rattled, and a nearby wind chime nearly sent me out of my skin as a breeze came whipping through the complex. Nothing else moved, but something wasn't right. I felt it in my gut.

A dozen or so slow steps and I was at my apartment door. It wasn't open, but it wasn't *quite* closed either, and I knew Clyde hadn't left it open. I stood there, ears straining for any signs of what I might find inside.

Nothing, dammit.

I exhaled, releasing the lip I'd absently caught between my

teeth. One last look around the complex and I used my free hand to give the door a gentle push. It caught on the carpet, opening only six or seven inches, but that was enough. Wynn stood in front of a shelf full of framed photos, holding Clyde.

"What the hell are you doing?" I demanded, pushing the door open farther. "And how'd you get in?"

He never even flinched at the sound of my voice. "Waiting for you. JoJo let me in. Said she'd give you a holler and let you know I was here," he replied, turning to face me.

"He bites." I stepped inside, cautiously scanning the room for any other hidden intruders.

"JoJo—"

"No, *Clyde* bites. I haven't spoken to JoJo this morning. Now, what are you doing here?"

"I've decided Cielo might be a nice place to start over, so I went to see JoJo this morning and rented an apartment . . . neighbor."

Bullshit! He was no more starting over than Clyde was. Whoever Wynn was and whatever he wanted, he wouldn't get it from me. 'Cause I'd be long gone by sundown.

6

The slack-jawed expression on Bonnie's face was worth the cost and inconvenience of taking up residence in Cielo's only apartment complex for a week, and not much more. Especially after the shock Wynn had experienced at the sight of golden-eyed Clyde lounging on the back of her ratty old couch and the photos of Karen and Kevin Lyons on the shelf behind him.

The bottom had fallen out of his stomach at the sight of the photos, and, more important, at the realization he'd slept with his quarry.

And he knew Clyde was a cat, not some mysterious kid she kept locked in a closet somewhere while she went barhopping. The little heart hanging from his collar said so, damn her.

Back to the matter at hand—Bonnie James looked *nothing* like Julie Burt.

He took a hard look at Bonnie, seeing a bit of a resemblance now. At the very least, they could have been cousins. Julie Burt was heavyset with supershort, bleach-blond hair, hazel eyes, lots of jewelry, chubby cheeks, and a round ass. Bonnie James had slender curves and long dark brown hair, bright eyes, no fake nails, and a real tan. He'd bet his last twenty dollars she'd also had plastic surgery. Not a lot but enough to shave ten years off her face, maybe an eyebrow lift, a nose job, and green contacts. Subtle changes he could easily pick up on now, just enough to fool him.

He'd fucked the woman he'd been sent to *persuade* information out of.

Wynn Collier was in deep shit, and someone was going to pay. Facing Julie with a bland smile on his face, he held up a photo. "Who's this?"

Served Julie right for making him think she had a kid.

"You're staying?" She scowled, the next sentence practically a shriek. "Start over at what?"

The sound of a nearby door opening and closing and footsteps propelled Julie to slam her own door. Wynn struggled to think of her as Bonnie. Julie was a face and a file, someone he'd spent more than a year searching for, but Bonnie was a person, a woman he'd slept with, but he seemed to know Julie so much better.

Clyde stood up, stretched, and jumped from his arms to investigate the green stains on Julie's work boots.

"Start a new life. Oklahoma City just hasn't been the same since my divorce." He bit back a grin as her eyes narrowed skeptically. Even to him it sounded like bullshit.

"You know, there's not a lot of jobs in Cielo." Julie uncrossed her arms and propped her hands on her hips, revealing the dark green tank top tucked under the sleeveless shirt she wore. Faded Levi's tucked into the tops of her boots hugged her tiny waist and caressed her hips.

"That's okay. Because you see," he said, replacing the photo, "despite my ex-wife's best efforts to clean me out, I've got plenty to live off of for a while."

"And once it runs out?"

Clyde had moved to the windowsill in order to watch the comings and goings outside and lash the air around him with his thick gray tail.

"I'm sure I can find something. A simple life doesn't require a lot of money, now, does it?" He gave her a sharp-eyed gaze, pleased to see her looking decidedly uncomfortable.

Eyes narrowed, she shifted from foot to foot, her fingers now jittery. She didn't like him invading her space, and he knew why. He plucked another photo of Karen and Kevin Lyons off the shelf in front of him. "How come there's no photos of you two together?"

"Because I was usually the one taking the pictures." She crossed the room, snatched the frame from him, and reverently placed it back on the shelf.

She was lying. He'd seen the photos his brother had taken of Julie's apartment after her disappearance. There were tons of pics of the sisters as well as Karen, her husband, and Julie/Bonnie. And old ones of the other sister, the one who'd taken off after high school, never to be heard from again. His brother, John, had tracked her down, and she was currently living the party life in Miami Beach. She didn't know anything. Had barely been moved enough to fly to Scottsdale to tend to her sister's estate or search for Julie . . . Bonnie . . . shit!

"When do you move in?"

"Tomorrow. Today. Whenever I want. I've already got the key."

She crossed her arms over her chest. "You go on vacation with furniture?"

"No, my mom's sending it." As soon as he called her and told her to, that is. "Busy tonight?"

"Look, Wynn, you're a nice guy, but you know I don't sleep with the locals, and you're now officially a local."

What the hell?! "You mean, now that I live here, we can't

35

have sex?" If he couldn't get close to her, he was sunk. If nothing else, he'd figured the one way to get close to Julie was to sleep with her, frequently. Like that was a hardship. Smiling, he said, "Surely you jest."

"I don't jest." Now it was her turn to look smug, damn her.

Time for Plan B, and damn he hated doing this, but he wasn't about to lose whatever tentative grip he had on her. "What if I told you I knew your secret?"

She turned white in the blink of an eye but didn't go so far as to sway on her feet or anything overtly girly, and she recovered quickly. "I don't know what the fuck you're talking about."

Wynn couldn't afford to spook her to the point that she ran. He moved closer until he could smell her sweat and plucked a piece of fresh-cut grass from her cheek. "My first night in Cielo I couldn't sleep, it was too quiet. So I went for a drive."

Her cheeks turned pink, and her eyes sparkled with something. Anger probably, or embarrassment. Pale and flushed wasn't a good look for her.

"I saw you looking in that window. I know what you were doing. I guess the question is, why? Watching porn would be so much less risky." His smile was meant to soothe, but he didn't think it worked too well on Bonnie. She was definitely on the defensive, and he got the feeling she preferred the offensive.

"Maybe I'm just a pervert. You always wander around in the middle of the night?"

"It wasn't even ten o'clock. So how long have you been watching them?"

"Who?" she asked, frowning. The pulse at the base of her throat was going wild.

"Whoever you were watching . . . how long?" he prompted.

"I have to get back to work." She flung the door open, ushering him out with an angry wave of her hand.

He followed at a much slower pace. "Maybe we can finish this discussion over dinner?"

"I don't cook."

She was lying again. He knew for a fact she used to be quite the gourmet cook. "I'll cook," he offered.

"I don't recall seeing any pots and pans hidden away in your hotel room."

Shrugging, he shoved his hands in his pockets and stepped out into the stifling heat before turning and giving her cleavage one last look. "My place, six o'clock, and don't be late."

7

Fucking pictures!

I'd made the mistake of believing I was safe out here in the middle of nowhere. I'd relaxed my guard more than I realized. Thought a few more days wouldn't matter.

If Wynn had gone digging, he could have found my other identities and some cash, carefully concealed behind some Sheetrock in the bedroom closet. Obviously he didn't want me dead, but I didn't intend to stick around and find out what he *did* want.

As soon as Wynn was gone, I headed for the bedroom closet, yanked out my suitcases, and threw one on the bed. The other I carted into the living room and threw open on the couch.

Fuck! Fuck! Fuck! I couldn't take the pictures with me this time. Not one.

Clyde's meow reminded me that I couldn't even take him. He'd be a dead giveaway to whoever came in Wynn's place. I guess I could leave a note, giving him to Wynn since they were such bosom buddies. I jumped at a knock on the door, then forced myself to relax at the sound of Tony's voice.

"I got the new linoleum for 5-B."

Sagging against the door, I pinched the bridge of my nose in frustration. "I'll be there in a minute."

"Everything okay?" He peered around my shoulder, his eyes widening at the sight of my suitcase, then focused his attention back on me.

"Yeah." We stared at each other for a few heartbeats, looks full of silent understanding.

"Going somewhere?"

"Yeah." I opened the door and ushered him in, something I'd never done. "Probably."

"Anything I can do to help?"

I scrubbed at the back of my head in frustration. "Um. Fuck! I can't explain. I just have to leave."

"I understand."

I'm sure he did.

"Store my stuff—like you would anyone who skipped out."

"Will do."

"Get started and I'll be there in a few."

I locked the door behind him, even though it wouldn't do much good; it hadn't kept Wynn out. Or rather JoJo hadn't. I didn't want to run, but there was no one to discuss my options with. I'd have to take my chances on the road, like before. But where would I go? I sank down on the couch. I couldn't go back to Scottsdale. I had no family except my sister, Lisa, and I wasn't even one hundred percent sure where she was, other than Florida.

I'd spent the first six months after Karen's death crisscrossing the country, spending time in libraries and Internet cafés researching people who lived off the grid, how to buy fake identities, and watching the aforementioned mob movies.

No, Karen wasn't killed by the mob. At least, I didn't *think* so. She and Kevin were killed by a gas explosion. And she'd known her life was in danger. Not that she'd bothered to tell me, directly, ya know? But she'd dropped enough hints the last time I saw her.

In hindsight, I couldn't be mad at her since I totally understood her fears.

Why did she run? All I remember of that evening was that we'd talked, reminiscing about the Fourth of July picnic. She'd pulled out a pic of Kevin and his best friend, Duane Huffsteder. Contemplated it. Duane's suicide a few days after the celebration had hit them both hard.

"How's Kevin doing?"

"He's scared."

"Scared?"

"Yeah." She sat silently for a few minutes, then slowly shook her head. "It wasn't a suicide."

"Karen"—I squeezed her hand—"he hung himself."

"No, he didn't! I don't know what he was into, but whatever it was, now Kevin's scared and talking crazy-talk. He's ready to quit as soon as we get back from our vacation."

"Scared of what?" His shadow? Shit, he was an accountant for a pharmaceutical company.

"Whatever Duane knew got him killed. Kevin seems sure of it."

"And now Kevin's involved?" I grabbed her arm, forcing her to face me. "Kevin's *not* involved, is he?"

Her head jerked up, her big brown eyes filled with fear. "I have to go." She lurched off the couch, her purse clutched to her chest.

I followed, unwilling to let her get away until I had more answers. "Karen, are you in trouble?"

"Be safe. And take care of Clyde for me!"

When the cops showed up a few hours later to tell me about the gas explosion, I'd freaked. I'd probably overreacted when I ran, but deep in my gut I knew their death hadn't been an accident. A growl from Clyde reminded me where I was and that Tony was waiting.

A few thoughts. Wynn seemed like a nice guy—for a stone-cold killer or whatever the hell he was. He didn't seem subtle enough to be the FBI, and he didn't seem like the PI type, not that I knew what the PI type was. He might just want information. He hadn't killed me yet, which meant he wanted something besides my head on a platter. Except, I had no idea *what* he wanted.

Maybe . . . just maybe I should find out.

I spent the day in 5-A with Tony, laying linoleum and being thankful for work that didn't really take a lot of concentration. Late in the afternoon, I went and got us some lemonade, wishing it were beer, wishing I'd spiked it with vodka, but the monotony of physical labor had helped work off some of my nervous energy. Other than cleanup, we were done. We settled on the floor, sweaty and grimy and happy to get off our aching knees.

"Running gets old," Tony said absently.

"I don't see any other way."

"Sometimes there isn't. Sometimes you stand and fight."

"Would you?"

"If I had something to fight for, yes. I've been lucky so far, but I also think there comes a time when your back's against the wall and you have no choice."

Fatigue settled deep in my bones. "I have no place to go, and I don't want to spend the rest of my life running."

"Then I think you'd better fight, sen'rita."

Fighting was all well and good, but it could mean my life. And I wasn't really ready to die. Granted, I pretty much already had. I had no life. I had no future, nothing to look forward to. I guess I really had nothing to lose either way I went.

8

Wynn headed up 67 North to Fort Stockton, home of the nearest Wal-Mart, while dialing his mom.

"How's it going, Wynnie-poo?"

"I need your help again, and you can't tell Dad." Wynn grinned to himself and blatantly ignored the use of his nickname. The thought of pulling one over on his dad, especially with his mom's help, tickled the shit out of him.

"What have you . . . wait. I'll help you, but you have to keep me in the loop. You know how your father is. He doesn't tell me anything."

He told her as much as he dared, including Julie's fake name, and wisely omitted that he'd slept with her. "If I push too hard, she'll run."

His mom chuckled on the other end of the phone. "She sounds like a clever girl, and you can't afford for her to run."

"But not clever enough to not be found." He sighed. "What if she doesn't know about her sister?"

"Is that what you think?"

"That's what my gut's saying." And no amount of persuasion from anyone would change that.

"Then why did she run? If she doesn't know her sister's alive, then Karen and Kevin are probably with the Feds, dear."

"Not according to my sources. I think they're on the run. Now, I need you to send me a bed and a couch, lamps, a few books, and some clothes. Doesn't matter what, it's just temporary, but I need to make it look good."

"I'll get to it in the next day or so. What's the address?"

He rattled it off and hung up, a smile on his face as he covered the last few desolate miles to Wal-Mart.

Two hours later, he pushed out a cart loaded with food, pots and pans, a cookbook, and an assortment of basic household goods, including an air pump and an air mattress. And a huge box of condoms. He wasn't dumb. A stranger in a small town seen frequently buying condoms wasn't the type of attention he wanted. And he had no intention of driving back to Fort Stockton for more anytime soon. Well, he would if he had to, but he didn't *want* to.

Grinning to himself, he set the cruise control and headed toward his new home, miles of sand and scrubby landscape sliding by.

How the hell did Julie stand it out here in the wilds of nowhere? Apparently, a girl did what she had to in order to survive. He could respect that even if he couldn't appreciate it.

Back in Cielo, he parked behind the complex and quickly unloaded the Blazer. Julie was nowhere in sight. That's okay. He'd be ready for her when she showed up after work.

He put the chicken on to boil, then set another pot of water for the noodles on the stove for chicken tetrazzini.

He hauled in the rest of his things, carried all the empty boxes and bags to the Dumpster, then finished their dinner and slid it in the oven. The apartment didn't look homey, or even romantic, but it'd do, and even without a bed, it was actually better than the motel. The sink and countertops were new, as were the plumbing fixtures in the bathroom and the tub. He had to give her credit. She did good work.

He stepped out of the shower to find the apartment filled with the smell of warm cheese and butter, and Julie taking the tetrazzini from the oven.

"Nice towel."

"Nice overalls." He shivered in the chilly air, his grip tightened on the towel wrapped around his waist. "How'd you get in?"

"Door was open." She tossed the pot holders on the counter and let her eyes drift down the length of him. She might as well have been touching him with those tiny, callused hands of hers. "You should be more careful."

"In Cielo?" He laughed, moving toward the bedroom door.

"Even in Cielo," she said softly.

He didn't miss her narrowed eyes or the thin set of her lips. Something wasn't right. And it was more than just him busting her about being a voyeur. "Duly noted. I'll be right back."

In the bedroom, he dug a pair of khaki shorts and a fresh polo shirt out of his suitcase, dressing as quickly as possible before rejoining Julie in the kitchen.

"So how was your day?" she asked.

"Good." He slid a loaf of Italian bread in the oven to warm. "Talked to my mom. She's sending my furniture."

"And she wasn't at all alarmed that her baby boy was moving to the middle of nowhere?"

"Mom understands I need to do what I need to do." That, at least, wasn't a lie.

He set the timer and opened a bottle of wine, pouring them both a glass. "Want some?"

"I'm more of a beer girl, but thanks." Once upon a time, she'd been a wine girl, a martini girl even, but he let it slide.

"So what about *your* mom?" he asked, even though he knew the answer. The question was a natural progression and hopefully wouldn't put her hackles up too much. "You two close?"

"She died when I was in college." She slowly eased away, turning and heading toward the living room window.

"I'm sorry." He wasn't really sorry. At least not in that I-didn't-know way of people who ask personal questions of people they barely know. "Were you close?"

"Not really. Sort of. It was a long time ago." She spun around to face him. "I think we need to lay some ground rules."

"Ground rules?" He took his wine and followed her into the living room.

"We can eat, we can talk, I'll even let you pet my . . . cat, but no third degree."

Shit!

"The place, it's got great charm."

He laughed ruefully. "You should see the air mattress."

"I'm sure it's almost as charming as you are." She turned back to the window, peeping through the blinds.

He ignored her dig. "Anything interesting out there?"

She just couldn't help herself, could she? Always looking, always nosing. Had the habit grown out of her paranoia after her sister's supposed death, or had she always been like this? Had her nosiness been a source of conflict in her sister's marriage or no? Had she protested her sister's marriage to a dull-as-dirt accountant who'd probably never be anything more? Who'd shackled Karen to a middle-class suburban hell? Then shackled her to a life on the run thanks to whatever he'd stolen.

"Maybe later we can test out the air mattress and see how sturdy it really is." He stood directly behind her, pressed against the length of her as much because he enjoyed it as he knew it would irritate her.

She couldn't move away without giving him a shove first, and she'd never show her discomfort at his closeness.

"How about no?" She released the blinds and gingerly maneuvered around to face him. "Where'd you learn to cook?"

No to sex was not good. Not good at all, and not just because he'd blown money on a supersized box of condoms either. He forced himself to focus, stay in the moment. "My mom."

"Are you a mama's boy?" Her expression was guarded enough to put him on high alert.

"Some would say so." Most notably his brothers and probably his father, though he'd never said the words out loud. "You know this isn't fair?"

"Huh?" she asked, sipping her wine.

"I can't ask you anything personal." He quirked an eyebrow, waiting to see how she'd respond.

"Them's the rules, babe. Take 'em or leave 'em." She jabbed a finger at the door, one eyebrow quirked in question.

"But it's my apartment."

"Fine." She set her wineglass on the windowsill and turned to go.

"Who you gonna peep tonight?" He smiled in triumph as her shoulders stiffened.

"Blackmail doesn't become you." She glanced at him over her shoulder.

If she only knew. "Blackmail is such an ugly word! Let's eat," he added as the oven timer started to buzz.

He turned toward the kitchen, sure she wouldn't leave and not just because of the blackmail. Whether she knew it or not, Julie wanted him. Wanted to be there, was probably tired of being alone.

Human nature dictated that man (and woman) socialize, gather, fuck, and hunt, not live alone like Julie had for the last three years. Only the old and sick were left behind, to die, and Julie was neither old nor sick, despite her—what the hell did you call a female Peeping Tom again? *Voyeur* would just have to do. Julie was lonely, whether she'd admit it or not, and he had every intention of taking advantage of that fact.

"Hope you brought your appetite!"

She joined him in the kitchen, leaning against the counter. "Meet any of your neighbors?"

"Just the hot blonde downstairs."

"Big tits, nice tan?"

"Sounds like her." He stopped fixing their plates to top off her glass.

"Her boyfriend, Tan—"

"Tan?"

"Yeah, Tan, good-looking, Oriental guy. They fight 'cause he thinks she's cheating, but he can't catch her."

"And?" he asked, waiting for the punch line.

"She's sleeping with their roommate."

"That's not right."

"I dunno." She shrugged, a smirk on her face. She was enjoying this. "Tan's sister's kinda hot."

Pot holder clutched in his fist, he stared at her in shock. "She's cheating with his sister?!"

Julie giggled. It sounded rusty and hoarse, as if she hadn't laughed in a long time. As if she never laughed anymore. He filed that away for future use. Humor was good, and he had a feeling sly humor worked especially well with Julie.

"No wonder poor Tan can't catch her . . . So, exactly how hot is his sister, and do I even want to know just how *you* know they're, yeah, ya know." Wynn shrugged.

"I walked by their window once, and they were making out on the couch."

"Where was Tan?"

"At work I guess." She shrugged. "You gonna interrogate me about your new neighbors all night or feed me?"

9

I didn't trust Wynn. I didn't know his game. I just couldn't bring myself to trust someone that Clyde liked. After all, Clyde hated me, which just went to show what a poor judge of character he was.

Plate and wine in hand, I sank down on the floor with my back against the living room wall. Wynn definitely had money, and he'd apparently spent a ton outfitting his apartment today. He'd gone to a lot of trouble to make this look good. That's where I should start. "What'd you used to do?"

"Real estate and some investments." He smiled from his spot back against the built-in bookcase. His long-ass legs were stretched out in front of him, his size 12 feet crossed at the ankles. He was long and lean and, damn me, I liked that in a man. That and the sound of his voice—deep and smooth. Under different circumstances, I might even call it soothing.

"So how many siblings do you have?" I picked at my food, which, by the way, was better than anything I'd had in a long, *long* time. Cooking for one sucked.

"Three. Two brothers and a baby sister. Dani's kind of a

princess." He shrugged and smiled in a way that said he liked her that way and maybe she was even his princess, in the way older brothers can do.

"You mean she's a spoiled-ass brat?" I challenged just to see what he'd say.

"If by spoiled-ass you mean inviting the entire sophomore class over for a pool party on her sixteenth birthday, yeah."

"I assume it wasn't a small class."

"And she got a BMW. It was just a three series and used, but it was better than Will, John, or I got."

"Jealous?" I teased, even though I knew he wasn't. You could tell by the twinkle in his eye. And he was telling the truth. He really did have a sister. Probably had two brothers also.

His mouth full of tetrazzini, he shook his head no.

"So, what did you get your sister for her sixteenth birthday?"

"Wet. I threw her in the pool."

The mental picture of him picking up his cute, willowy sister who probably had his blue-green eyes, and her screaming while he swung her around had me hiding a giggle behind my wineglass.

The guy was good, damn him.

"And I got in big-ass trouble too."

"How old were you?"

"Twenty and home from college. She got me back, though. Two years later, she set me up on a date with one of her friends. Six months later, I married her, and here I am."

"You were married for fifteen years?"

Wynn just didn't strike me as a man who'd been married that long. I mean, you could just *tell*, for Pete's sake! Married people just *looked* different. And acted different too. Scowling, I watched him have a choking fit. Once he recovered, he got us both more wine and sat beside me. Uncomfortably close, even.

Close enough so that (a) I couldn't look at him and (b) we were bumping elbows as we tried to finish our dinner. Nice stalling tactic.

"We didn't live together for most of it."

I couldn't help myself. "So why did you—"

"—stay married?"

"No. Finally get a divorce."

"She met someone."

"Let me guess, another woman?"

"No, actually, it was another man," he said, nodding slowly. He didn't sound like he'd minded either.

I would have apologized except he didn't sound like a man who . . . wait a minute. "She left you for another man, she barely lived with you, *and* she cleaned you out."

"No"—he pointed his fork in my general direction—"she *tried* to clean me out. I've found that, for the most part, rich women are just flat out greedy."

"Even your mom?"

"Mom is the exception to *every* rule."

Smiling easily, he raised his wineglass, and I did likewise even though I had no mom and hadn't in quite some time. And when she was alive, she'd been a total pain in my ass, nagging at me to get married like Karen had. And, Jesus, that turned out well. Well done and crispy.

I snorted softly, then realized, or remembered, I wasn't alone at home on my couch. I was sitting here with Wynn. Sometime soon I'd have to bust him for hunting me down.

And I knew just how to do it.

10

Wynn sat on his air mattress in his darkened bedroom, sipping wine and waiting on Julie to make her move.

Her sudden departure after dinner had left him worried she planned to bolt sometime in the night, and he had to stop her, at all costs. The security light from outside illuminated the landscape with a pale yellow glow broken by the deep slash of shadows.

The stories about his sister, Danielle, had worked like a charm, but he'd nearly fucked up saying he'd never lived with Kelly. They had, in fact, eloped his junior year of college and promptly gotten a divorce five short months later, something her daddy had paid her handsomely to do. It was a lesson learned, and Wynn didn't waste time on bitterness.

Across the way, the lights were out in Julie's apartment, but still he waited until she finally came slipping out her apartment door. Much to his relief, she was empty-handed. Maybe she was just going on another peeping expedition. Or maybe she was going to move her truck. With one last glance out the blinds, Wynn stood and hurried to the living room window.

Even from inside, he could hear the slight rattle of the stairs as she made a slow descent. He forced his anxiety down and waited, watching her circle the pool. A quick glance at his watch assured him it was only just after ten. She stopped to talk to the old man across the way before continuing her walk, finally disappearing from view.

Wynn slipped out his own front door, checking to see if she'd doubled back before he descended the stairs.

As quietly as possible, he circled around the side of the building, listening for the crunch of her shoes in the dirt before he moved any farther. There wasn't a lot of light here thanks to the pine trees between him and them and despite his best efforts, he couldn't get a read on Julie's location. He should have known something was up when he didn't hear any footsteps, but he'd attributed it to Julie just walking quietly. She hadn't been walking; she'd been waiting, as he found out when something solid connected with the side of his knee.

He went down hard, white-hot pain radiating up his leg, making his stomach tighten and his eyes tear up in shock and pain as a body settled on his chest and pinned his arms to the ground.

"Hi, Wynn." Julie tossed aside the aluminum bat she'd nailed him with. It clattered sharply against the asphalt, setting his teeth even more on edge.

She was cutting off his oxygen supply, and between that and the pain, he could barely think.

Fuck! How the hell had he underestimated her? He knew how. He'd been thinking with his dick, assuming he could charm her, woo her for what he wanted. The girl had gone to a lot of trouble to stay hidden; she'd be smart enough to pick up on someone following her and going into her apartment. Invading her space had been a huge miscalculation on his part.

Stupid dick! "How you doing, babe?" he panted, trying to breathe through the pain.

"I've been better. How's your knee?"

"Hurts like a motherfucker," he ground out.

She leaned down until they were nearly face-to-face. "What the fuck do you want from me?"

"I was just wondering where you were going."

The weight on his chest increased; her thighs tightened on his arms, the rough pavement digging into his back. "Liar. If you wanted to kill me, I'd be dead already. So what do you want, Wynn?"

Fuck! *Fuck!* "Information," he panted, sucking as much air as possible through his nose. "That's all. Just information. I'm not a killer."

"How do I know you won't go back and tell your hit-man friends where I am?"

"All I want is to know where your sister is, and I'm out of here."

"I haven't spoken to Lisa in years."

"Not Lisa. *Karen.*"

"My sister's dead. Thanks to one of your little friends, I'm sure. And I saw your face. Now you have to kill me. That's how it works."

He would have laughed but he couldn't because of her weight on his chest. "She's not dead. And I told you, I'm not a killer. But in—"

"Liar! The police said they found two bodies!"

"She's not dead. WITSEC was supposed to take her and Kevin in, but they died. Or appeared to. They're not. I swear to you, Karen's *not* dead, but your life's in jeopardy, and probably Lisa's, too, if you don't help me."

His bomb had the desired effect; she relaxed from the shock

of hearing the news. He bucked, sending her flying over his head, and had her on her back pinned under him. "I'm not a killer, but in five or six days, one will be here if you don't help me. And he's not nice."

"Friend of yours?" she gasped. Then sniffed. Shit, she was crying, goddammit!

"Brother." He winced, cursing his stupidity again. His knee hurt from the sudden movement. "Look, I'm sorry about your sister—"

"Right, *fucker.*"

"I have to find her. Her husband, Kevin, has something that doesn't belong to him."

"Is that why they tried to kill her?" Now she was struggling for air, her chest huffing. Her tears were about to turn into a full-blown crying jag.

"They didn't. I think your sister staged a suicide."

"Why the fuck—?"

"Who the hell knows, but she worked in the morgue and she had free access to all the John and Jane Does she could want. The bodies were burned beyond identification."

"Then where is she?"

"We don't know. If I let you up, you promise not to run?"

She glanced up at his arm pinning her hands above her head, then back at him.

"I like you. I don't want to hurt you, Julie."

"My name's Bonnie. Bonnie James."

"Your name is Julie Burt." He released her hands, slowly struggled to his feet, and held out a hand to help her up. "I've been hunting you for nearly eighteen months."

Her expression guarded, she accepted his help, immediately releasing his hand once she was on her feet, then crossing her arms over her chest.

"Let's walk." A hand at her back, he led her between two

parked cars to the middle of the parking lot where they had more room. "Have you had any contact with Karen?"

"No."

"If you had, would you tell me?" He grinned in the dark, not surprised when she said no again. "I believe you. Do you have any clue where she and Kevin would go?"

"Up till five minutes ago, I thought she was dead! How the hell am I supposed to know where she is?" She spun away from him, then turned, giving him a shove that knocked him off balance and made his knee spasm in pain. "And why the hell should I tell you anything?"

"Because if you don't, a very bad man is going to come and put a gun to your head, pull the trigger, and dump your body in the desert for the coyotes to pick apart. Then they're going after Lisa, and eventually they will find Karen and Kevin. Do you want that? Huh?"

"No."

"Look, I know you're tough. I know you're smart, and I know you can handle yourself, but the only way to save your life—"

"Is to help you find my sister so your brother can kill her and Kevin?"

"Not exactly an ideal situation, I know. For what it's worth, I just want what they have. I don't want to hurt them . . . or you." He couldn't be any more honest than that.

"So you get what you want and just go away?"

"Yeah."

"Bullshit!" She shoved him again. Enough to set his knee to hurting again.

Enough to piss him off so he'd shove back. Then he got her upper arm in a vise grip and dragged her to his apartment, slamming and locking the door behind him before he finally released her. "Don't go anywhere."

He limped to the kitchen and filled a bag with ice, then rejoined her. She stood with her back to him, peeking out between the blinds much like she'd done earlier.

Finally, she turned to face him, the fear in her pale face obvious under the lamp's 60-watt bulb. "You really aren't going to kill me?"

"I'm not a killer, but my brothers and father are."

She snorted softly. "Aren't you the big disappointment?"

"You have no idea." He sank down on the floor and held the ice on his knee. He knew that put her above him, but he figured she needed to feel in control right now. The last thing he wanted or needed to do now was scare her into running.

"So, how did you end up the white sheep of the family?"

Laughing, he said, "Mom."

She sat silently a while, then said, "What do we do now?"

"We find your sister. I've tapped some sources, so I know for sure they're not in witness protection. That means they're out there somewhere. We find them, we get the evidence from them, and we help them and you get out of the country."

"Why are you helping me?"

"I'm not even supposed to be telling you any of this, let alone *helping* you. Most of the time, I go after people who get what they deserve. Know what I mean?" He continued after she nodded. "That's my job. People like you and your sister and Kevin *are not my job.*"

"Okay?" Her voice was low and hoarse. She looked stunned and shaken.

He felt bad for her, but they didn't have time to waste. She was strong, resilient, and she'd make a quick recovery, because deep down inside, she knew she had to.

"You're taking this awful well," he said, laughing.

"I think I'm still processing. You have any of that wine left?"

"A little." He made to get up, but she waved him down and helped herself.

"Want some?"

"No. I better not. Julie, I hate to push, but tell me what you know about the night you thought Karen and Kevin died."

11

"To be honest, not a lot." Back from the kitchen, I sank down beside Wynn, still trying to process the fact that my sister and brother-in-law were alive. "Karen came by after dinner to drop off Clyde. They were going on vacation. Well, they *said* they were going on vacation, but they'd been acting weird for a while."

"How long?"

"Couple weeks. Just after the Fourth of July." I took a big sip of my wine and licked the traces of it off my lips, trying to recall as much as I could as quickly as I could. "I just chalked it up to a friend of theirs committing suicide."

"And?" he prompted. "Where did she say they were going?"

"Grand Cayman on some cruise out of Florida—"

"Where your sister is."

"Lisa?" I breathed. "I haven't seen her since Mom and Dad died." Hadn't talked to her either.

"She's there. My brother tracked her down. Said she could barely be bothered to go to Scottsdale and settle your sister's estate."

"I'm not surprised." I shook my head. Lisa was a major head case. "Karen said that things weren't going well at work for Kevin and that he really needed this vacation. She said Kevin was afraid and that he was giving notice as soon as he got back. It was almost like she was hinting, so when the cops showed up a couple hours later, I freaked out and ran. Does Lisa think I'm dead too?"

"Technically, you're just missing. There was even talk for a while that you were involved with your sister's death, but that went away pretty quickly. From what I read, the whole thing came under *a lot* of scrutiny from the police, though, before it just died out."

"From what you read?"

"I'm the third person they've sent after you, honey."

"Do you know what they're looking for? Why they'd want Karen and Kevin dead? They blew up their house! Was that one of your brothers?"

"My brothers don't deal in explosives. Too messy. I don't have all the details, but I'm almost positive your sister did it."

"Why?" Indeed, it boggled the mind, and the wine coupled with the adrenaline from nailing Wynn in the parking lot didn't help. "Why?" I asked again, because I didn't know what else to say.

"Kevin has something that belongs to his employers, Sunset Pharmaceuticals. And he had to have been in pretty deep for them to go to such extreme measures. They want it back, soon."

"How soon is 'soon'?"

"A little bit less than two weeks," he admitted.

"So how do we find them?"

"Tell me everything you know about your sister. From the beginning."

I talked all night. I talked until I didn't have a voice anymore, and I couldn't think of one more thing to tell Wynn, and the sky outside was turning pink. I talked because I had no choice. I still didn't trust him—not a hundred percent anyway—but I had to find my sister, and he had to help me. If I ran, he or someone worse would find me. I had nowhere to go anyway. Obviously not even Canada would be safe. And I had no one but Wynn to turn to.

I glanced at my watch. "Fuck. I can't believe it's nearly six."

He struggled to his feet and limped into the bathroom. I scrubbed at my face with the palms of my hands as fatigue sunk in deeper and stood up, scrounging around his kitchen to make coffee. Thank God he'd bought a coffeepot.

"Can I ask you something?" I said once he joined me again.

"My knee's fine, thanks."

I laughed but didn't apologize. He'd put me in jeopardy and gotten *exactly* what he deserved.

"Why are you helping me?"

"I told you. I don't usually have to hunt . . . normal people. And if I find what Kevin took, I'm in my dad's good graces again."

"What about . . . afterward?"

"We can still see each other but no getting serious on me."

I rolled my eyes in obvious disgust and got some milk out of the fridge for my coffee. "I meant what happens to me and my family?"

Smiling, he reached for two cups and set them on the counter beside the pot of coffee that had almost finished brewing. "My orders were to find you and, through you, retrieve what your brother-in-law took from his employer. That's it."

"So, theoretically, they could send someone else to finish the job. Afterward."

"Only if they can find y'all."

Which meant, one way or another, I'd spend the rest of my life on the run. I halfheartedly toasted him with my coffee cup.

* * *

Spending the day doing apartment remodeling wasn't my idea of fun, especially after being up all night with Wynn. I felt wrung out, drained, and numb by the time I joined Tony in 5-B.

"You're still here."

"For now," I said. If it looked like things might end up going south, I'd disappear again, and this time leave the country. I'd go to any country. Didn't matter; it wasn't like I'd broken any laws (yet) and would have to face extradition. I'd just have to find a country that would let me bring Clyde. I smiled. *Karen* would have to find a country that would let *her* bring Clyde; me, I'd be shed of that damned animal, if we managed to get out of this mess. "You want to tackle the tub or start on 8-A?"

8-A was one of those things that you ignored and hoped would go away, like a plus sign on a pregnancy test or a big zit on prom night. The tenants had trashed the place, then moved out in the middle of the night, taking only their clothes. Just cleaning it up enough so that we could do make-ready would take two or three days. But the tub in 5-B had to be refinished, and I hated the smell of epoxy.

"Never mind. I'll do the tub," he said, smiling in understanding.

"You don't have to," I offered, thinking damned if he didn't. "I'll take the tub."

Early that afternoon, Wynn found me standing in the middle of 8-A cursing everyone who'd ever lived here, all their ancestors, their pets, and their pets' ancestors too.

I was hot and sticky, and I'd only trashed out half the apartment. With me going in and out, I'd shut the air off, so my jeans and T-shirt were stuck to me along with ten layers of grime. I yanked off my yellow rubber glove and accepted the icy can of

Coke he handed me, swallowing half and burping. I flashed him an apologetic smile. "Sorry."

"Why security deposits were invented." He blinked a few times at the pungent odor.

"No shit?"

"You need a biohazard suit," he said, looking me up and down. "This is a long way from commercial real estate, lady."

"Exactly how much do you know about me?"

"Pretty much everything," he said, sipping his own drink.

"What happened to my house . . . and stuff?" I figured since he knew everything, he was the one to ask all the questions that had bugged me for the last three years.

"I think your house was foreclosed on. Since you're not legally dead, there wasn't much else Lisa could do."

"And I guess making the payments was too much to ask. I hope your day was more productive than mine."

"I've been cooking a brisket all day."

"Well aren't we just the happy cooker." Sue me for being grouchy. I was entitled after the last twenty-four hours.

"Get cleaned up and meet me for dinner, and we'll talk."

"How's your knee?" I asked as he turned to go.

"Better."

I still wasn't apologizing. "I'll see you about six?"

"You can't knock off early?"

"Unlike some folks, I don't get paid on commission or anything," I said, giving him a pointed look.

"Fine!" He held up his hands in surrender, an apologetic smile on his face. "I'll see you at six, then."

As Wynn left, Tony arrived with JoJo hard on his heels. She was dressed head to toe in red. Even her Ariat Fat Baby's were red. Her wispy, pale blond hair was pulled back in a semblance of a French twist. If I didn't miss my mark, she was going dancing in Alpine tonight.

"If you'd spend more time working and less time flirting, this'd be done by now."

And if she'd spend less time shopping online, we'd have more money to fix the apartments up. "Did you need something, JoJo?"

"Just came to check up on you since I hadn't seen you around. Thought maybe you'd snuck off for a nap."

Shit. *One mistake and she never lets me live it down.* Bitch. "Maybe if you'd open your blinds, you would have seen me trekking back and forth to the Dumpster with those forty-pound sacks of garbage."

"The bathtub's done, so I can help," Tony said. His way of keeping the peace, which he was really good at and was part of the reason I liked him so much.

"See," I said, waving a hand in his direction, "we'll be done in no time." Yeah right. We still had at least a day's worth of cleaning in here.

Her nose twitched, then seemed to almost shrink on itself. "What's that smell?"

"Cat." I pointed to the mask positioned on my head. It didn't help the smell much, but God only knew what else was floating around in here I couldn't see.

"They never paid a pet deposit." Shaking her head, she turned toward the door.

"Genius," I muttered as she walked out.

"I heard that."

12

"I'm starving," Julie said when he swung the door open.

If there was one thing he'd learned about her, it was that she wasn't one to waste words. "Come on in. It's all ready." He led her to the kitchen and handed her a plate. He'd do whatever was necessary to butter her up for what he needed *her* to do. To that end, he'd spent the day cooking brisket and making homemade potato salad. He'd even done up a relish tray with two kinds of pickles and driven all the way back to Wal-Mart to get some Kalamata olives for her.

They chatted about boring unimportant stuff while he made her plate and poured her a glass of wine.

"You don't have any tea?" She held up her wineglass.

"Not in the mood?"

"I got a headache from being in that damned stinky-ass apartment and, of course, I was up all night."

"I guess that didn't help." He retrieved another glass from the cabinet and filled it for her. "I'll give you a massage after dinner."

"And then what?" she asked with a grin. "Because I'm not sleeping with you again."

"And then we'll see." He fixed his own plate. "As long as you promise not to run off."

"I can't leave Clyde alone all night. He'll tear shit up." Turning toward the living room, she said, "I fucking can't wait until we find Karen, and I can give her that damned cat back."

Laughing, he joined her on the floor. He'd talked to his mom earlier, who'd assured him his furniture and some more dishes would arrive tomorrow. He hadn't told her his cover had been blown. She'd only fret. But they had talked a lot about Julie and Karen . . . and Lisa.

The more he thought about it, the more he believed Lisa was the missing link in all of this. Her distance from her sisters and her somewhat shady connections was the perfect cover-up to help Karen and Kevin get a new identity and get lost. However they'd done it, they'd been super-sneaky about it, because he'd found nothing to connect the two sisters. It figured that the least obvious of the sisters was possibly the most involved.

"I talked to my mom again today."

"And?" she said around a mouthful of potato salad. "Damn, this is so good." She sagged against the wall and chewed, a tiny smile of pleasure on her face.

"Thank you. We went over everything my brother John had on Lisa. There's nothing to outwardly connect her to Karen and Kevin's disappearance."

"Told you. The bitch is crazy."

"Sure it doesn't run in the family?" he countered. From what John had said, she was wild, she ran with a rough crowd, she had a record and probably a drinking problem, but she wasn't necessarily crazy.

"Ha-ha." She stuck her tongue out at him, then popped an

olive into her mouth. The smile on her face was worth the two-hour drive back to Wally World to get them.

"Anyway, there's a big but in there. My gut says she is connected. Tell me about Lisa. Tell me what John *doesn't* know."

"She got kicked out of high school for selling pot—shit, Wynn, that was over ten years ago. To be honest, I don't know her any better than John or you do."

"Try again," he urged. "Where does she fall in the pecking order?"

"Youngest."

"So she's spoiled. Likes to have her way."

"Yeah." She shrugged. "I guess."

"She's only three years younger than you. How can you not know your sister?"

"Karen was the brain, I was the fat one, and Lisa was the beautiful spoiled one, okay? That's how we were raised. You could find us in any Psychology 101 textbook. She got kicked out of high school, and two weeks later, Mom and Dad were killed in a car accident. I was going to move home from college and help out, but Lisa took off right after the funeral."

"I need you to call her."

She forked up another olive and popped it into her mouth, chewing thoughtfully before answering. "Right. I'm gonna call up my estranged sister, who probably thinks I'm dead, and ask her if she's heard from our dead sister. If I were her, I'd definitely think someone had a gun pointed to my head."

"Not everyone watches *CSI*, Julie."

"*Law and Order*," she corrected.

He nearly choked on a mouthful of brisket. "Whatever. You have to call her. Be honest. Tell her you're looking for something, and under no circumstances is she to tell you where Karen and her husband are. If you don't know, you can't tell and that means I can't tell either. And she needs to play it cool. If John even thinks that Lisa knows something, he'll go after her."

"Would he hurt her?" she asked. She looked wary, afraid, and dark circles had formed under her eyes from fatigue.

"Probably," Wynn reluctantly confessed. He didn't want to make things worse, but he had a feeling that, at this point in the game, she'd appreciate the truth, no matter how bad, a lot more than she'd appreciate more lies. "John is ... um ..." How exactly did you tell someone your brother made his living killing people?

"What?"

"He ..."

"Just spit it out, Wynn. Is Wynn even your real name?"

"Yes, it is, and I screwed up even telling you. I'm human; sue me."

Her expression was painfully serious. "I'm gonna die, aren't I?"

"Not if I can help it. But John and Will aren't exactly the nicest guys in the world. Lemme try that again. My dad still hasn't forgiven me for not going into the family business."

"Which is?"

"Knocking people off."

"Knocking people off what?"

He didn't mean to laugh; it wasn't funny, but he just couldn't help himself. "The planet."

After dinner, they headed to the Speedie-Mart, located on the highway that led out of town, to use the pay phone. Wynn bought them a couple more sodas and got a couple dollars in change.

"I shouldn't have eaten so much."

Actually, she hadn't eaten that much. It was nerves, but he

left her alone about it. The last thing he wanted to do was set her hackles up and have her balk at the last minute.

He handed her the quarters and dug through his folder for the phone number. "Ready?"

"As I'll ever be." She sighed.

Once they were through, he'd take her home and make sure she went straight to bed. More than anything, she needed some rest and it showed.

"If you want, afterward I'll buy you an ice-cream cone."

"Very funny, asshole."

While he read them out, she punched the buttons with shaky fingers, then added more quarters when the recording came on the line. "It's ringing." She licked her lips, turned her back to him, then turned back to face him again. "Answering machine."

"Leave a message. Tell her you'll call her back in an hour."

She did and once she'd hung up, made him make good on his ice-cream offer. "I binge when I'm nervous."

"Let's go." Hand on her back, he guided her to the Blazer.

"You know, she sounded just the same on that recording," Julie said in between licks of her ice-cream cone.

He watched her tongue lap up ice cream, then scolded himself. This wasn't the time to be thinking about sex. "Is that good or bad?"

"I'm not sure." She sighed and flicked off a chunk of the chocolate coating with her tongue, drawing it into her mouth. "Probably bad considering she's twenty-eight."

"Ready to head back?"

"What's the rush?"

"We can sit outside the convenience store and eat there as easily as we can here." He pointed the Blazer back toward the store.

"Fine. So what kind of car do you really drive?" Her free hand caressed the dusty console between the seats.

"BMW."

"Seven series?" She sounded more than a little wistful, reminding him once again of how much she'd given up in the last three years.

He pulled into the parking lot, stopping directly in front of the phone and killing the engine.

"Maybe when this is all over, I'll let you take it for a—is that phone ringing?"

They were out of the car at the same time, Julie tossing her half-eaten ice cream on the ground as she ran. "Hello! Lisa?"

Wynn stood to the side, pen and paper in hand, ready to scribble down any tidbits Julie threw his way. When she tilted the handset so he could listen, he leaned over and pressed his head against hers.

"It's Jules, and I don't have much time."

"Jules! Oh my God! Holy freakin' shit! Where the hell have you been?"

"I'm safe," she stammered. "Are Karen and Kevin? Did you know?"

"Hell yeah, I knew. Fuckers were after Kevin, and if your silly ass hadn't disappeared, you'd have known that."

"Wait, Lisa, let me talk. Are you sure this line is secure?" Julie asked, glancing in his direction.

"No way to know, so keep it short," he murmured.

"Who the fuck is that?" Lisa demanded, her voice suddenly all business. "And where the fuck have you been?"

"It's okay. I promise, but I don't want to say too much, and we need to keep it short. If . . . if folks find out you know where I am, you could be in danger."

"Jesus H. Christ, first Karen, now you! And Mom said I was the reason she had gray hair."

This was no laughing matter, but Wynn was forced to pull away from the phone and catch his breath, relieving the ache in his sides brought on from holding it in before he rejoined Julie. "Lis! Pay attention! He's here to find something. I can't tell you who he is; you just have to trust me. He says if he finds what he's looking for, he won't have to find Karen and Kevin."

"I don't know if I should say anything more," Lisa drawled, her voice now distant and distrustful.

"I understand."

Wynn took the phone from her with a reassuring smile. "I want to do this in a way that'll keep your sister and brother-in-law safe, Lisa."

"Sure." She sounded far from convinced.

"See what you can do and we'll give you a call back tomorrow."

" 'Kay, hey call me back at this number."

Wynn juggled the phone while he scribbled, then repeated it back to her. "Here's Julie."

With one last look at Wynn, she spent a few more minutes reassuring Lisa that she was safe, and, no, she didn't need any help going underground, before she hung up. "Lisa said she doesn't know, only that she heard them talking and it's in a safe place."

He wasn't surprised Lisa had given Julie more than him, and even though what she'd given her had been little, it'd been enough to give Wynn hope that they'd be able to see this through with as few complications as possible.

"Good, that's good." He squeezed her shoulder.

13

Talking to Lisa had been harder than I expected and all I wanted was to get away from Wynn, to be alone, to feel a little normal again, even though deep down inside, I knew my life hadn't been normal for a very long time. After he dropped me off, I headed up to my own apartment and sank into the couch, forcing an unhappy Clyde onto my lap.

He scowled up at me, blinking those ugly yellow eyes, then turned to lick his shoulder. Don't ask me how I knew it was a scowl. I just knew.

Eventually, he worked his way free, sprawled on the carpet, and proceeded to clean his privates. "Eww."

I lurched to my feet and stepped outside. Sleep would be a long time coming, and a walk was in order. At least that might make me feel slightly normal.

Downstairs, Tara was splashing around in the pool with her latest hoochie-boy. They changed as often as she changed her nail color, which was often. "Hey, Bonnie, wanna join us?"

I wandered over to the security fence and leaned against it.

Her "friend" was cute. I had to give it to her, Tara had good taste in men. "What happened to What's-His-Name?"

"I got a new What's-His-Name!"

And apparently lost her bikini top again. With a shake of my head at the sight of her B-cups, I turned away, ready to go for my walk, when Wynn appeared at the top of the stairs. I slowly circled the pool and met him at the bottom.

"If you want to be alone, just say so."

"I'm good." I considered kicking him for being so damned understanding. Instead, I stuffed my hands in my pockets and headed for the walkway between the apartments.

"So, who we watching tonight?"

I shushed him, then silently dragged him down the walkway to the parking lot. "Darcy's husband is home," I whispered.

"So that guy you were watching her with?"

"Brad, the town mechanic."

"Has he ever changed your oil?"

"Jealous?" I laughed.

"No way." He wrapped an arm around my shoulder and pulled me close. There was something comforting and familiar in it, something I hadn't had in a long time.

"Will I ever have a normal life again?" I asked as we walked.

"Sure you will. Soon as this is all over, you can relocate someplace nice like Brazil—"

"Fuck you!" I said, shoving my elbow into his side. "I don't speak Portuguese."

"Ouch! I thought they spoke Spanish."

"That's what you get for thinking. It's Portuguese, baby."

"Who we peeping on tonight?"

"*Nobody!* Now keep your voice down."

"Why do you spy on people?"

"Euh!" With a curl of my lips, I looked him up and down. "Why are you a thug?"

"Kaylee and Tan had another fight."

What?! Was he trying to tempt me with gossip or something? "I know. It's a really small complex, in case you didn't notice."

"You could slip him a note and tell him who she's cheating with."

"That's mean. And Tan's a nice guy, so no way"—I shook a finger in his direction—"and don't you either! When's your furniture going to get here?"

"Mom said tomorrow."

"So your mom really did send you your stuff?"

"Some of it. Obviously, I'm not really planning on staying here any amount of time."

"Aw, now. Cielo's not so bad when you get used to it."

"Not exactly my idea of a good time either. I've got a house in Dallas already, but I'm not there much. Work keeps me on the road a lot. I promise not to trash the place, but I guess I can kiss my deposit good-bye." He grinned at me, his teeth gleaming in the moonlight.

My belly did a funny little flip-flop thing brought on from more than an overindulgence in ice cream. Let's not get carried away, though. Wynn was the closest thing I'd had to a real friend in three years, and he got paid to beat people up—or whatever. Not exactly Nobel Peace Prize material. But I was feeling off-kilter, to say the least.

Sue me for feeling vulnerable. I was tired mentally, physically, emotionally. After everything that had happened in the last twenty-four hours, after living a lie for so long.

At least with Wynn I knew where I stood. At least with Wynn there was no pretense. I turned to stand in front of him and let my hands glide up the length of his chest to encircle his neck.

His head dipped ever so slightly; then he whispered, "This is a very bad idea."

"I know."

He gently pushed my hair away from my face, tucking it behind my ears. "You sure?"

Thanks to the fucking lump in my throat, dammit, I couldn't speak. A nod would just have to do. I buried my face in the softness of his shirt, inhaling the woodsy scent of his cologne, his warmth and maybe even a bit of his strength, and gave in.

He silently led me to his apartment and slowly undressed me. It was the first time since losing all that weight that I felt shy around a man, afraid to speak, out of my element. Afraid if I spoke, the reality of what we were doing, the lines we were crossing, would be too much.

We stretched out on the air mattress, both of us laughing softly at the silliness of it; then we were touching each other, communicating silently. Kissing softly. Wynn's tongue gently exploring my mouth, teasing me, warming me, his fingers between my thighs, gently stroking me, making my clit swell, making me wet.

His cock was pressed against my leg. Then I was on top, with Wynn buried deep inside me. The security light outside cut through the blinds, lighting our way. Illuminating his hands on my breasts, his fingers tweaking my nipples and caressing my stomach while I rode his cock, plunging up and down, my lip caught between my teeth. I wanted to scream and cry, beat on his chest, but I didn't want the neighbors to hear me.

He moaned, his hips moving with mine, our pace quickening as his fingers slipped lower to tease my clit, his cock stretching me, filling me with every stroke while my clit swelled with every stroke of his fingers until Wynn finally spoke.

"Hurry."

It was my pleasure to pick up the pace until my orgasm shot through me, heat and sweet release searing me from the inside out. I collapsed on Wynn's chest, still unwilling to speak as awareness returned. A light dusting of hair on his chest tickled my cheek and moved with every breath I took, but I couldn't bring myself to move, and Wynn apparently wasn't in any hurry to make me.

Late the next afternoon, I sat on the steps leading to the second floor watching two burly men carry the ugliest couch created by humanoid life-forms upstairs to Wynn's apartment. It was a work of blue velvet art. You know the kind, with huge-ass flowers, overstuffed arms, cute throw pillows, and a matching chair. It would never be considered Shabby Chic, but it might qualify as Shabby '80s. At least it wasn't brown. It, along with the dresser, bed, brass and glass tables, and *luscious* gilt mirrors—pardon me while I pull my tongue out of my cheek—made quite an ensemble. Someone had a wicked sense of humor. When I'd toasted Wynn with my soda can earlier, he'd flipped me the bird, obviously not nearly as excited as I was about how his happy abode was shaping up.

At least he'd have a bed for us to use now.

Even though I knew sleeping with Wynn was a bad idea, the thought of having him in a real, live bed again got me to my feet and back in 8-A to finish up trashing it out.

Having a semisteady diet of sex had made me hornier than a sixteen-year-old boy on Viagra.

It's just a saying, so don't get bent.

But after going without for a while, you sort of got used to it, just like you sort of got used to *having it again.* And, can I just say, it's much easier to get used to it than *not.*

Once the movers were gone, Wynn joined me in 8-A. Tony was out fixing the A/C in Darcy's apartment. The units were water-cooled and occasionally froze up.

"Did you call your mom and thank her for all that nice furniture?" I smirked, yes, I did.

"Yup, and I'm giving it all to you when I leave."

I held up a dirty, gloved middle finger, then knotted the bag I'd just finished filling. "I've got to mop, and I'm done for the day. What's for dinner?"

His lips quirked in a crooked little grin, and he propped his arms on the door frame, stretching his faded Shiner Bock Beer T-shirt across his chest. "Awful sure of yourself there, girly."

"I've been down here busting my ass all day. The least you can do is feed me." I tossed the bag next to the other ones stacked just inside the door.

"Oven-fried chicken. One hour and don't be late."

One last pat of the door frame and he turned toward the stairs. I followed, setting two bags of trash outside the door and pausing to admire Wynn's ass a few more minutes.

Grinning under my mask, I turned toward the sink with a renewed burst of energy. Thirty minutes later, I'd Lysoled the entire kitchen, mopped, and was locking up when Tan came storming out of his apartment, bags in hand, slamming the door behind him. I wasn't touching that situation with a ten-foot pole.

I headed upstairs, assuring my grumbling tummy we'd eat as soon as I showered. Clyde was not going to be happy at being left again.

The apartment was better than I expected—or worse, depending on your point of view. "Your mom has great taste in furniture."

Wynn scowled at me from his spot at the oven. He'd centered the couch in a place of honor on the wall where I usually sat to eat and had hung the matching gilt mirrors over it. The brass and glass coffee and end tables were obviously second-hand and slightly tarnished, but everything was clean and, in some perverse way, kind of homey. I guess the smell of Parmesan and chicken helped.

"If you want to eat, I suggest you be nice to me."

"If you want, I can bring Clyde down here and let him scratch everything up for that touch of authenticity." Smiling, I closed the door and dropped my keys on the coffee table.

Honey, I'm home, flitted through my head. There was, actually, something nice about having someone take care of me. I'll admit to feeling a bit awkward being back here after last night. A bit; not a lot.

I crossed to the sink and washed my hands while he put the finishing touches on our dinner. Besides the chicken, there were Italian-style green beans with garlic and tomatoes, a loaf of fresh bread, and a huge salad. "Can I help?"

"Nope."

He never wanted me to help. Which was also actually kind of nice. "I *can* cook, you know."

"I know." He handed me a plate heaped with food and nodded toward the kitchen table. "Sit."

I took it and sat, sipping my wine while I waited on him to join me. "You like being all domestic, don't you?"

"Don't tell anyone, but I'll make some woman a fine wife someday." He sank into the chair opposite me, his plate piled as high as mine.

"That's hysterical, Wynn. A domestic enforcer. Boy, I feel sorry for your kids."

"I would never be hard on my kids." His statement was dry and very matter-of-fact.

I'd overstepped myself. "Sorry. Guess my sarcasm got the best of me."

"S'okay. You know," he said, pointing his fork at me, "I have a theory. Would you like to hear it?"

I stared at him for a few heartbeats, then grunted, "Sure."

"By the time I was conceived, poor old Dad didn't have enough testosterone in his swimmers. So I got a lower dose than my brothers."

"And then you got a sister," I added with a laugh. "You do have a sister?"

"I have a sister, and she's exactly like I said she was." His lips twisted into a smirk. "A total brat."

"Y'all are close."

"Literally and figuratively. She lives about ten minutes away from me, and she comes over whenever her roommates are driving her nuts, partying too much, or she needs to study."

"She's still in college."

"She's taken the slow track."

"That must be kind of weird. Growing up in a family that . . . you know."

Wynn chuckled softly and ran a hand through his hair. "She's definitely the tenderhearted one. And whenever she gets mad at Dad, she gives money to charity on his credit cards. Sometimes it's lots of money." He shrugged in a way that made me think he liked his sister's quiet rebellion. "Dani is the only person who can get to Dad."

In the space of just a few short days, Wynn and I had somehow managed to fall into some sort of pseudo-couple routine, cemented after the night on his air mattress. Shortly after we finished up the dishes (together), we headed for ice cream and the pay phone so I could call Lisa back.

Someone named Candy answered the phone, rattled off yet *another* number to call, and hung up. I never even got to ask any questions or run the number past her.

It was all very *X Files*.

With an eye-roll in Wynn's direction, I slipped more change

into the phone and dialed the new number, praying I'd memorized it correctly. With change in one hand and ice cream in the other, there'd been no way to write it down.

"Lis—" I'd barely gotten the words out of my mouth before she started speaking.

One short sentence was all I got before she was gone again. I stood there, the dial tone buzzing in my ear, staring at Wynn with what had to be a shocked expression on my face. It felt shocked, and judging from the frown on his face, it was. I slowly replaced the phone in the cradle, then licked the dripping ice cream off my hand.

"Well?"

"Lisa said I have what you want."

14

Wynn stared at Julie, feeling as shocked as she looked. His heart actually slowed down for a few heavy beats, and he almost dropped his ice cream. The feel of sticky, cold goo dribbling across his fingers had him pitching the remains of his sugar cone into the nearby trash barrel. This was not good.

"Anything else?"

"No." She frowned, her head dipping thoughtfully, her eyebrows pulling together the tiniest bit.

He reached out to give her a reassuring squeeze only to stop and lick the sticky remains of his dessert off his hand first.

"All she said was that I have it. Then she hung up. Do you . . . have to tell . . . people?"

"No, baby, absolutely not." He took her ice cream from her, threw it in the trash with his, and pulled her to him, suddenly feeling incredibly protective.

No way in hell was he telling anyone that Julie had what Sunset wanted. No way was he letting his brothers, or his dad for that matter, get their hands on her.

"We have to find it," she murmured, her head buried in his chest.

The question was, *how.* "Let's go to my place and talk."

Back at the apartment, he gently shoved her down on the couch and poured her another glass of the merlot they'd had at dinner. She downed half, blinked, and seemed to visibly pull herself together again.

"What do you have of your sister's over there?" He sank down beside her, draping an arm across her shoulders.

She snuggled closer before answering. "Pictures." She sighed. "The night she died, she brought me photos from their annual Fourth of July picnic, including the framed one you had the day you broke in."

"What else? Negatives maybe?"

"No . . . no negatives. They were taken with a digital camera, and she didn't bring any."

"The picture frame is a possibility, but it'd help if we knew exactly what we were looking for. You said she brought you Clyde to watch the night she died, right?"

"Yeah."

"Cat carrier. Was he in a cat carrier, Julie?" He forced himself to breathe, to relax, to ease up on the sense of urgency that ate at him.

"Yeah!" She brightened considerably and leaped up, obviously intent on searching for the carrier and photos, only to plop down beside him again, looking as glum as she had when they'd gotten home. "What if it was in the bag of food?"

He blew out a long heavy breath. "Surely your sister wouldn't put something that important in a bag of cat food. Come on." He stood and offered her a hand. "Let's get this over with."

Outside, the night sky was dark and empty, and a dry breeze rattled nearby trees. On the street below, the clang of a can blowing by, beating an erratic tattoo on the asphalt, could just be heard over the hum of the air conditioners.

Clyde heard them before they saw him. He sat in the open window of Julie's apartment, greeting them with a low growl.

"Stuff it, Clyde." Julie shoved a key in the lock and pushed the door open, flicking on the light as she went. The cat barely let her get three steps before he was winding his way between her legs, making all kinds of cat noises.

If Wynn didn't know better, he'd swear the furry little shit was actually trying to trip her. "Clyde, kitty."

At the sound of Wynn's voice, the cat turned, crouched, and jumped into his arms. He was actually kind of cute, except for those freaky yellow eyes.

"Shut the door so he doesn't get out, please."

Clyde dug his claws into Wynn's chest, trying to get free when he realized his avenue of escape was disappearing. "Sorry, buddy," he said, giving the cat a scratch under his chin.

"Don't let Satan there fool you, sugar. He's a killer." She turned around, her lips twitching as she realized what she'd said.

"Maybe when all of this is over, we can give him to my dad as a gift."

"A killer for a killer. Now that's fucking funny." Julie moved closer and reached out to scratch Clyde's back, but he wasn't having any of it. He lunged from Wynn's arms, barely missing her on his descent, and disappeared around the corner with the scratch of his claws on the linoleum.

"He really does hate you."

"It's fairly mutual. Wynn?"

"Hmmm?" he asked, heading for the photos on the entertainment center. Some of them were gone. "Where's the rest of the pictures?"

"I packed them up."

Understanding dawned, and he took a quick hard look at her. "You were going to run the other day, weren't you?"

She nodded ever so slightly, and even though Wynn knew just how strong and capable she was, at that moment she looked incredibly fragile. An illusion, nothing more. She'd survived worse. Julie wasn't the type of woman to crack under pressure, which was good.

"Wynn?"

"Yeah?"

"How are we going to find it if we don't know what *it* is?" While she talked, she dragged a suitcase from the closet beside the front door and gently set it on the couch. Inside were the rest of the photos.

"That does complicate things, doesn't it?" He quickly took the frames apart and searched them thoroughly, but he found nothing.

Whatever it was, it had to be small. Small enough to be taped to the back of a photo or the inside of a frame or slipped into an envelope of photos and not be noticed.

He dug his cell phone out of his pocket and speed-dialed his mother. "Can you talk?" He glanced at Julie, who watched him warily as she continued to inspect the last few remaining frames.

"I was hoping you'd call. How's it going?"

"I got the furniture, thanks. And, um, things are—"

"Are you in trouble, Wynnie?"

"No, Mom. I just need a little help."

"Please tell me you didn't lose Julie, honey."

"I didn't lose Julie, Mom."

Julie giggled and he turned his back on her, taking the time to study the photos again while he talked. "Dad never told me what it was Kevin Lyons took, other than 'evidence.' Do you have any idea?"

"You know he doesn't talk business with me."

"And you still manage to keep tabs on everything us boys get into."

"Yes, dear, and as I remember, your father sent you to find Julie and get information from her so your brothers could find her sister and brother-in-law. Not you."

"It's not that simple, Mom."

"Yes it *is*, dear. If she says she doesn't know where they are, then you just make her tell you. Wynn, don't screw this up."

"She doesn't know, but we did find—"

"*We?* WYNN! You didn't! Please, tell me you didn't do what I think you did."

"She"—he lowered his voice—"found out."

More soft laughter behind him made him wish maybe he hadn't been so hasty in calling his mom.

"Wynn! You should come home. We'll send Will."

"It's too late for that, Mom. Now would you just listen? If you don't know what I'm looking for—"

"Julie. You're looking for Julie and Karen and Kevin. *Find them.*"

"Mom! It's too late for that. Find out! Whatever it is, Julie apparently has it. Don't ask how I know, and *don't*, under any circumstances, tell Dad. Call me back when you know something."

"That sounded productive," Julie said after he hung up.

"She's worried," he said, turning to face her. Her green eyes twinkled, her lips twitched, and her eyes looked suspiciously damp. "So you think that's funny?"

"Well . . . yeah." She drew her legs up and hugged them to her chest. "Mama's boy."

"I got your mama's boy, honey," he said while crossing to stand in front of her. He held out his hands. She grasped them and he hauled her to her feet. "Want to go back to my place and try out my new bed?"

She did that funny little thing where she pushed her lips to the side and examined the logo on his T-shirt. "We could just stay here, since, you know, we're *already* here."

"True." His hands slid lower, into the waistband of her shorts, cupping the round globes of her ass. "Got condoms?"

"Do birds fly?" Grinning, she slipped free and led him toward the bedroom. Like the rest of her place, it had that thrown-together, impermanent feel with just a bed, a rickety nightstand with a dollar-store lamp, and a battered, secondhand dresser. Simple, utilitarian, with not a touch of female fuss anywhere. Not that Julie was the type for fuss, but it was sad.

She pulled a few condoms from the dresser drawer and waggled them at him before tossing them on the bed. "Did your mom know?"

The last thing he wanted was to think or talk about his mom right now. He shook his head, then yanked his T-shirt off. "No, but she's supposed to try to find out."

"What do you do when you're not . . . working?" Her eyes skimmed over him from head to toe.

"I work out. I play golf. A little tennis. And I swim." While he talked, he crossed the room, his pace deliberately casual.

Julie backed around the side of the bed, a coy smile on her face, and sank down on the edge, crossing her legs underneath her.

"What about you?" He took a seat beside her and leaned in enough to make her uncomfortable. As much as she wanted him, Julie *still* wasn't sure about having him around. That was okay; he could deal.

"I . . . lift deadweights," she said with a shrug.

The trash bags. Chuckling softly to himself, he leaned in, skimming his lips up the length of her neck. She shivered the tiniest bit, her head drifting to the side and giving him better access.

Her hand was on the inside of his thigh, sliding under the edge of his shorts and causing his cock to swell and tighten painfully in anticipation. He pushed her down onto the bed, lifted her shirt, and leaned over, planting his lips just above her belly button. She shivered again, her stomach trembling, her hands pushing him out of the way as she struggled out of her shorts.

He lifted her shirt over her head and knelt between her thighs, inhaling the sweet, slightly musky scent of her through her bikini panties while his fingers traced a path up the back of her calves. He followed with his tongue, pausing to suckle at the back of her knee, then turned his attention to her pussy, drawing his tongue across the fabric covering her clit. She surged against his lips, moaning loudly, her fingers digging into his scalp.

Wynn pushed her legs upward, slid her panties off, and draped her legs over his shoulders before diving in. She was soaking wet, her pink clit jutting upward, begging for him to play with it. He blew on it, and she shivered, arching against him again, silently wanting more. He traced his tongue over it, slow long strokes reminiscent of her with the ice-cream cone, until her legs tightened, her heels dug into his back, and she rose off the bed, urgently pushing her clit against his tongue at a pace more to her liking.

"Fuck . . . fuck . . . fuck me, Wynn."

He quickly sheathed his cock with a condom and threw her legs over his shoulder again, driving into her. She was like a starving woman underneath him, bucking and heaving, clawing at the sheets as he slammed into her. He couldn't catch his breath; he struggled to get more air in his lungs, to rein himself in before he hurt her, but she wouldn't let him slow down. She wouldn't let him stop until she came again, her fingers furiously strumming her clit. He shifted her legs, burying his face in the pillow to muffle his shouts as he came, the furious pounding of his hips reduced to sharp thrusts. Then, finally, his heart slowed and he could breathe again.

They both lay there, still connected, slick with sweat.

Wynn pressed a kiss to her damp temple, pushing her hair out of his way. "Damn."

"Baby," she drawled, "that's the understatement of the year."

15

It'd been three years since I'd woken up next to a man in my own bed. Even the other night I'd left after Wynn had fallen asleep. To say it was disconcerting was an understatement. Part of the reason we normally stayed at Wynn's was just so I could leave. Not that he knew that.

And last night things had definitely taken a turn for the more complicated.

I ignored the urge to dive under the covers and wake Wynn up with a blow job, slipping out of bed and grabbing some clean underwear. From the bedroom floor came the sound of his cell phone ringing.

If I was smart, if I had any sense of self-preservation at all, I'd ignore it. I glanced at the bed. Wynn apparently slept like the dead, because the muffled chirping hadn't disturbed him in the least. I tiptoed back across the carpet and grabbed his shorts, then left, shutting the door behind me. The readout on the phone's caller ID told me nothing except that it was a 405 exchange. It meant nothing to me.

I shouldn't. I really shouldn't. But I did it anyway, hoping, if nothing else, to get a better idea of what I was up against. No matter what Wynn said, I was still afraid someone would come and finish his job for him, and I wasn't ready to die yet.

"Hello." I dropped his shorts and headed for the bathroom, closing the door all but a crack.

"Who is this?" It was a woman, an older woman, and judging from her voice, not a happy one. Had to be Wynn's mother.

"Bonnie James." I wasn't about to give her my real name, even if she did know who I was.

"Is Wynnie there?"

Wynnie? Oh, he was so not ever *living this one down!* "He's asleep."

A sigh of possible frustration or motherly angst filled my ear. "You're playing a very dangerous game, dear."

"Did you find out what we're supposed to be looking for?"

" 'We' is it? I did, and I'm not happy. You tell Wynn that when he wakes up."

"Sure." *Or not.* I grinned at my reflection in the mirror. "Is there any other message, or are you going to call back?"

"I shouldn't tell you this. I shouldn't even tell *Wynn* this. It's his job to do his job, but I am his mother, so I'll give him a few points for . . . being so motivated. I hope you're worth it, honey. Sunset Pharmaceuticals was trying to pull a fast one on the FDA. They lied about clinical trials on a new cholesterol drug, and not just a little bit either. Your brother-in-law has proof and they want it back before the drug hits the market."

"But Kevin was in accounting." My reflection frowned back at me, and I shivered in the chill of the air-conditioned bathroom. How the hell had a number cruncher gotten himself in so deep that someone wanted to kill him?

"I don't have all the facts, but there's reason to believe a friend of his gave it to him."

Duane Huffsteder. No wonder Kevin and Karen had been so upset over his "suicide." "Anything else?"

"I think that's enough, don't you, dear?"

Sometimes I was glad I didn't have a mom. "Later."

I snapped the phone closed, slipped it back into Wynn's shorts, and kicked them just inside the bedroom door. He hadn't moved, despite the fact that Clyde had joined him on the bed while I'd been on the phone.

I spent most of my shower trying to figure out how the hell Karen had slipped me the proverbial Mickey and then run like the fucking wind. Damned if she hadn't left me holding quite a bag. Soon as this was all over, I was heading for Miami, and then for Karen so I could kick her ass and give her that damned cat.

By the time I climbed out of the shower, Clyde sat at his food bowl munching down on a can of something gross, and Wynn was standing at the counter, sipping coffee and watching him.

"How do you like your eggs?" He had a skillet on the stove and a carton of eggs next to it. "There's no bacon but—"

"I don't eat bacon," I said, circling around him for my own coffee. "It's full of nitrates."

"Duly noted."

I sipped at my coffee to buy myself some time. I shouldn't have snapped at him. "A fried egg sandwich?" I asked, smiling up at him.

He smiled back, leaned over, and kissed me on the cheek. The whole scene was scary in its domesticness. I had to go to work, and he had to do whatever he was going to do all day, then cook me dinner. I wanted to laugh but didn't. "Your mom called."

"You answered my cell phone?" His voice rose with each

word; he turned around, my cheap blue spatula clutched in his hand, his face a dark red.

"Yeah."

"What if it had been my dad, Julie?"

I winced, unprepared to be shouted at so early this morning. "He wouldn't have known who I was."

"He's not dumb, honey. He'd have known all right, and we'd both be up shit creek!"

"Okay! I'm sorry, all right. Shit." He did have a point. But then I'd known all that when I answered the phone. "She found out what we're looking for—well, sort of."

I quickly relayed our conversation while he fried up my eggs and made my sandwiches, adding cheese and extra butter. Real butter, none of that fake stuff. If I kept eating like this, I'd be back up to a size 18 in no time.

"Did she mention what format this proof was in or any other clues to help us find it?"

"No." I bit into the first sandwich, almost scalding my tongue and finger with runny egg yolk in the process. "But I think she might want you to call her."

"I bet."

While Wynn fried up his own breakfast, I got dressed and braided my hair. The second thing I was going to do when this was all over was cut this damned hair off!

"So?" I licked a bit of butter off my fingers and picked up half a sandwich. Wynn paused, his own breakfast halfway to his mouth, and quirked an eyebrow at me. "Wynnie." I gave him the cheekiest grin I owned and let it hang between us like a dirty diaper for as long as I dared. "Does she call your brother Willie?"

"And Johnny, and if you ever tell a living soul..." He stared at me, his expression deadpan, and let *his* reply hang between us like a dirty diaper.

Yes, I know I already said that.

"It'll be our little secret. I do have to wonder, though—what does she call your dad?"

"Poppa," he said, his face breaking into a huge grin.

I called it a day at four that afternoon and headed back up to the apartment. I needed, and wanted, time alone to go through the things Karen had left me, hoping I'd see something Wynn hadn't. After a shower, I started with the photo frames, taking them apart and setting them on the coffee table. Armed with a lamp, sans shade, and a magnifying glass, I went over every inch of the frame, the back of the photo, even the glass and the cardboard insert that kept the photo from slipping around. Nothing struck me as unusual or out of place. The cardboard was corrugated, though, so I carefully pried it apart in case Karen had slipped something in one of the little grooves. No luck.

But she *had* made a big deal out of it when she'd dropped it off. At the time I'd thought it was strange. I mean, I had dozens of pictures of the three of us, taken at various times since their marriage, including one of me at her wedding in the maid-of-honor's dress that I'd left behind—the photo, not the dress. After the explosion, I'd chalked it up to her saying good-bye.

Next I went through every photograph with the magnifying glass, searching for something stuck to one of them, or even something *in* a photo. The only thing that stood out was the presence of Duane Huffsteder, the friend who'd committed suicide. He didn't appear any different from any other time I'd seen him. And I couldn't recall anything about him and Kevin at the barbecue that stood out.

Two knocks at the door and it slid open with a hiss as it grazed across the carpet. Wynn had apparently gotten curious about where I was. No one else would dare just walk into my apartment. "You coming for dinner?"

Clyde stood up from his spot on the windowsill and hopped down, forcing Wynn to step inside and close the door. I watched, fascinated as the little shit jumped up in Wynn's arms and set to purring like, well, like a normal cat. Just then, my stomach rumbled.

"Guess so." I stacked everything back up in neat piles and slid my flip-flops on.

We stepped outside and left Clyde behind, much to his dismay.

"Remind me and I'll send some chicken home with you."

So I wouldn't be staying the night tonight. I couldn't help but feel disappointed. "What's on the menu, boss?"

"Besides you?"

"Ha-ha." I rolled my eyes for effect and started walking without him. Hoping he enjoyed the view.

He quickly caught up, following me along the walkway to his apartment. "What do you know about the woman living next door to me?"

"Mrs. Bezzel? Not much. She likes old TV shows and that's about it. Why?"

"She keeps watching me," he hissed.

"You're probably the hottest thing she's seen since the Fonz." I laughed softly to myself at his disgusted grunt and stepped inside Wynn's apartment, pulling up short at the sight of roses on the coffee table.

They were in a vase decorated with a light green gingham bow, and they were pink.

Maybe he just bought them to brighten the place up? And what was that smell?

"Pork roast?" I whispered hopefully. My stomach was apparently pretty hopeful, too, because it rumbled, *loudly.*

"Yes, and those are for you," he added, pointing to the flowers.

Man, talk about a sucker punch. I didn't even *like* roses—but they *were* pretty, and it'd been a long time since anyone had . . . you know. "They're very pretty . . . thank you." I turned and smiled up at him, feeling bashful and awkward, which made absolutely no sense since we'd already had sex. More than once.

"There's a card too."

"Are you always so nice to the people you work with?" Yes, I picked up the card, gently peeling the envelope open. I was no fool. Or maybe I was.

He'd Hallmarked me.

At least he'd been smart enough to stick to Maxine and go for the funny instead of the mush.

"I'm never this nice to people I work with. Of course, I'm not usually sleeping with people I want information from. I just thought you could use a little cheering up."

"I didn't know I seemed so down." I was going to have to do better. Card in hand, I headed for the kitchen, slowly so as not to look like a pig.

"I just thought it must have been tough talking to Lisa and knowing Karen was out there. You've had a bad week."

"Can I ask you something?"

"Shoot." His lips twitched and so did mine.

I sank down at the kitchen table and watched him finish up dinner. "If you weren't a *you know*, what would you be?"

He turned and leaned against the counter, an expression that could only be called "slightly wary" on his face. "I'm not going to make excuses for what I do or tell you I'm some sort of noble thug who robs from the rich and gives to the poor. It doesn't work that way. I am what I am. And I get paid to do what I do."

"But you don't kill people."

"I don't have to, but I hurt people, Julie. And I'm good at it."

16

He should have seen this coming.

Being with Julie was almost like getting into a new relationship. Well, it *was* a new relationship but normally . . . *normally,* he dated women who understood the kind of family he came from, the kind of life he lived, or he dated women who didn't care. Rarely did he venture outside of those circles, because it was difficult—no, almost impossible—to explain.

And he'd forgotten that when he'd allowed himself to get tangled up with Julie Burt. She would definitely care, and in her position, she wouldn't be able to separate the man from the job.

Because she *was* the job. Something he'd almost lost sight of.

"You okay?" Her soft question pulled him back to the kitchen.

He hoped like hell she couldn't see how much he regretted getting so close to her. The last thing he wanted to do was hurt her. "Don't think because I'm domesticated that I'm some sort of misunderstood thug or that there's some deep, altruistic meaning to what I do. There isn't. It's just a job. Now, do you still want to stay for dinner?"

She visibly paled. It hurt too much to look at her anymore, so he turned his back, grabbed a plate from the cabinet, and shifted the roast onto it.

"I do love a good pork roast."

His lips twitched; he sucked in a deep breath to stop himself from laughing. Leave it to Julie to cut to the chase. She was nothing if not resilient. And smart. If she could play the game a little longer, then so could he. "Then you'll love mine."

Pot holder in hand, he pulled a sheet of oven-fried potatoes, a perfect golden brown that made his mouth water, from the oven and set them on a trivet. "What were you doing when I stopped by?"

He set the roast on the table, then filled a bowl with the potatoes and joined her.

She filled both of their glasses from the pitcher of raspberry tea on the table. "Going through the photos again. In case we missed something."

"Any luck?" He motioned for her plate, filling it while she talked.

"No." She sighed, sipping at her drink. "I wish I could talk to Karen or that she'd told Lisa more about what we were looking for!"

"So do I, but any more contact could put your sisters in danger. We've got to accept that we're on our own here if we want this to all end well." And more than anything, he really did want things to end well. Julie and her family had been through enough. They deserved to live out their lives without fear that someone would find them when they least expected it.

At the sound of his cell phone ringing, Wynn rolled over and fumbled around, pawing at the nightstand until he found it. Clearing his throat, he flipped it open and pressed it to his ear.

"Where are you?" The sound of his brother John's voice was

as rude a wake-up call as a glass of ice water dumped on his head.

"Good morning to you too." Wynn tucked the pillow under his head and wished like hell he'd checked the caller ID first.

"After you called me about Lisa Burt, I decided to take a closer look at her. Our little party girl is gone. And guess what I found when I checked her phone records? A call from West Texas. Know anything about that?"

Wynn could almost picture the steam coming out of John's ears. With a soft groan of frustration, he sat up. "Where are *you*?"

"*I* am in Miami ready to board a plane for Oklahoma City."

Where Dad was waiting. They both knew it. Neither of them said it. They didn't have to. The last thing he needed was for his brother to talk to his dad, and for his dad to find out he'd had any contact with Lisa before she disappeared. The threat of his father hung over him like a scythe, ready to chop his head off.

"I'm in West Texas—"

"Did you tip her—"

"No. But you've got to give me my allotted time, John." He wouldn't beg. Not to his brother. He'd never be allowed to live it down if he did.

"Dad's counting on you, Wynn. You fuck this up and—" He faked the sound of Wynn's throat being cut. "If I go home, I have to tell him you contacted Lisa and now she's gone."

"Dad's not the only one counting on me. Now, if you can't help your brother out, at least give me time to wrap this up."

"What do you need?" He sighed. In the background, Wynn could hear the chatter of too many humans and someone calling out a coffee order.

"What the fuck are we looking for?"

"We? Wynn, what the fuck are you doing?"

"John?" he warned.

"Proof that—"

"I know it's proof!" Jesus Christ, it was like pulling teeth to get anything out of anyone. "In what format?"

"A microchip. You're looking for a microchip."

"Have a safe flight home." He hung up and sat there, elbows propped on his knees, phone dangling from his hand.

"Is everything okay?" asked Julie from behind him.

He lay back down, snuggling against the warm length of her, despite the tempting scent of coffee coming from the kitchen. He debated for all of three seconds on whether to tell her about her sister. "Everything's fine. Except . . ."

She sat up, a worried expression on her face, and drew her legs to her chest. "What is it?"

"That was my brother, John. Lisa's gone, and he knows we talked to her."

"Will he tell your dad?"

"I"—he shook his head—"I don't think so." As long as Dad didn't ask John directly. And Dad would if he found out John had been in Miami. John wouldn't lie, because he was unable to.

"What do you mean, you don't think so?"

"He's like fucking George Washington. He can't lie."

"You're kidding."

"Afraid not."

"I dunno, honey." She sighed. "A hit man who can't lie doesn't seem very effective."

"He doesn't talk much."

"But you don't know. You don't know anything for sure, do you?" she accused.

"I'm doing the best I can." He threw back the sheet and headed for the bathroom, hoping a shower would buy him some time to think.

A few minutes later, she joined him, taking a seat on the edge of the tub and letting in a blast of chilly air when she pulled the curtain back. "I think I should leave."

"Pour me some coffee before you go, would you?" He ducked under the spray to rinse the shampoo out of his hair.

"I mean, I think I should just take off. Wynn, we're never gonna find it."

His stomach clenched at the thought of what would happen if she ran. The idea that John or Will or even some stranger might track her down and execute her left him feeling weak-kneed.

"Hold up." He quickly finished up and shut off the water. "If you leave, I leave with you." He half-stepped out of the shower and angrily yanked her up by the arm. "You can't afford to run, and, more important, I can't afford for you to run."

She jerked away, landing against the towel bar with enough force to bring tears to her eyes. Or was she just crying? "Fuck you! And fuck your dad! Fuck your fucking reputation and your . . . your *job*! Fuck all of this, goddammit. I gave up my fucking life for this . . . shit!"

She stormed out, with him hot on her heels, *after* he grabbed a towel and draped it around his waist. Unfortunately, he didn't catch her until she made it just outside the front door. "It's okay," he said, his slippery fingers barely catching her arm.

"Fucking no, it's not!" Her words bounced off the empty, early morning courtyard like thunder, and next door, the volume of his neighbor's TV dropped drastically.

"Yes, it is. Now calm down and come back inside." While he spoke, he did his best to maintain his grip on her, but one wet hand was no match for her, and she easily got away.

Across the way, Old Homer's blinds were now open and Julie's coworker stood just outside his front door, calmly buttoning his shirt while he eyed Wynn. A toddler, dressed in only a diaper and socks, came tumbling out the door and clutched at his father's leg. Somewhere below Wynn, another door slammed. He couldn't follow her dressed in only a towel.

They'd attracted attention they didn't need. He quietly stepped back inside his own apartment and shut the door. In the bedroom, he dressed as quickly as possible, hopping up and down as he slid into a pair of sweatpants. At best, two, maybe three, minutes had passed. Not enough time for Julie to pack and get the hell out of Cielo. He snatched his keys from the kitchen counter and with one last wistful look at the pot of coffee, headed to her apartment.

His knock was answered by Manuel, Juan . . . *Tony.* Wynn could hear Julie in the bedroom, yelling something about what a bastard Wynn was and how someone was going to kill her if she didn't leave. He pushed the shorter man inside and slammed the door behind him. He was ready to push past him again when Tony pulled a .22 from behind his back.

"You don't want to do that," Wynn said softly. A chill that had nothing to do with his wet hair moved through him.

"You're right. But I will if I have to. She's family; you're not."

Julie appeared behind him, and a growl came from under the couch. "Tony, no."

The Mexican never moved.

"Tony, I don't need this kind of attention, and I'd bet you don't either."

"She's right. You shoot me and a cop will have you in handcuffs before she hits the city limits." Wynn moved closer, but Tony backed away, the gun leveled at Wynn's gut. Gut shots were bad—very bad. If you had to get shot, the gut was one of the last places you wanted to take a bullet.

"Go pack," Tony said, never taking his eyes off Wynn.

"I'm leaving, Wynn, and there's nothing you can do to stop me."

"Maybe not, but I guarantee if you walk out that door, I can't help you anymore, and the next man who comes after you *will* kill you, plain and simple. Then they'll hunt down Karen, Kevin, and Lisa, and kill them too." He hated strong-arming her, but he had no choice.

He'd do whatever was necessary to keep her from running.

"I don't think so." Her expression grim, she wandered closer but still outside the line of fire. "You see, you're going with me, and Tony, too, and he's going to shoot you, and we're going to dump your body in the desert down by Big Bend. Maybe even in the park. I figure your family will be too busy looking for your body to worry about me. And if, by chance, someday they do find me, it's not like I have any sort of life in the first place, now is it? I disappeared once. I can do it again."

"You can't take the cat. He's a dead giveaway."

"Tony will keep him for me."

"Where will you go?"

"Like I'd tell you?"

"You're just going to kill me anyway. You might as well."

"I'm not that dumb, Wynn."

Clyde chose that moment to come out from under the couch, but before Julie could scoop him up and throw him in the cat carrier, he ran for Wynn, leaping into his arms. "I don't think Clyde wants to live with Tony."

Her eyes narrowed to tiny slits. "I'll send him to your dad, then."

"Julie, let me help you." He moved toward her, only to stop at the sound of the hammer being drawn back.

"Put the cat down, Wynn."

"I won't let you do this."

111

"She said put the fucking cat down." Tony's eyes narrowed, and his stance was firm but relaxed, his accent almost undetectable.

Wynn didn't doubt for a moment that, given the chance, the other man would shoot him. But from the sound of sirens coming nearer, he wouldn't get the chance to. There would be no trip to the desert, no bullet put in the back of Wynn's head or anyplace else—today. "I suggest you ditch that gun before the cops get here."

Tony glanced at the window; those few precious seconds were enough for Wynn to pitch Clyde in his direction and make a break for Julie, who darted into the bedroom with a shriek. "Run, Tony!"

The front door slammed about the time she landed on the bed, and Wynn followed, pinning her down face-first. "You've put us in quite a jam with the cops coming here."

"So fucking go ahead and kill me already," she ground out, struggling against the weight of him on her back.

"I'm a lover not a fighter, darlin'." Even though there was nothing funny about the entire situation, Wynn couldn't hold back a grin.

If Julie had seen it, she probably would have decked him. He had to give her credit for having some balls, though. Or he would have if Clyde hadn't chosen that moment to sink his teeth into Wynn's bare foot.

"Ow! Fucker!" He lashed out at the teeth sunk in his toe, kicking Clyde loose and rolling over to grab his foot all in one motion. Clyde dove for the closet. "Motherfucker bit me!"

Next to him, Julie shrieked with laugher. "Fucking got what you deserved, asshole." She gave him a shove that nearly sent him flying off the bed and disappeared in the hallway. Her suitcase slid past the bedroom door as a knock echoed through the apartment.

Wynn stayed put, his foot clutched in his hand, blood welling from the tiny puncture wound. He hoped like hell Julie wouldn't tell the cops he was here. He really couldn't afford to be on anyone's radar. Pinching his big toe between his thumb and finger, he hobbled across the bed and leaned closer to the window and listened.

"Hi, Dan."

"You okay, Bonnie?"

All Wynn could see from between the blinds was a brown uniform and a gun belt.

"I'm fine."

"Mind if I take a look around? Your neighbor downstairs was pretty concerned when she called. She said something about a man chasing you and yelling."

Wynn pushed to his feet and exited the bedroom, ready to bullshit his way right out of a ton of trouble. "Who's at the door, babe?" He limped into the living room, forcing a sheepish grin onto his face for the deputy's benefit.

"It's Deputy Travers, *honey.*" She shrugged and sort of half-heartedly waved toward the door.

"Dan, please," the deputy said, shouldering past Julie, his hand outstretched to shake Wynn's.

Whoever had thought up the word *beefy* had done so with Dan Travers in mind. He was beefy and blond and making google-eyes at Julie while he fondled the gun strapped to his hip.

Coincidence? Wynn didn't think so. If Julie hadn't looked so irritated, he might have been jealous instead of struggling to control his laughter.

"Wynn Coldwell," he glibly lied. "I'm really sorry about the disturbance. We had a fight," he said, drawing the deputy's attention back to him. "Bonnie here got mad and threw the cat at me."

From behind the deputy's back, a narrow-eyed Julie snickered, her lower lip caught between her teeth.

"Is that true, Bonnie, honey?" Travers spun around, a frown of concern puckering his forehead. "You threw that old cat a'yours at him?"

Wynn didn't doubt the deputy slept with his gun, and possibly did other things with it too. Wynn waggled his eyebrows at "Bonnie, honey."

"I knew I'd left his claws in for a reason."

"Aw, come on, baby"—Wynn couldn't hold back a grin— "I'll take you to Alpine for lunch if you just say you forgive me."

"You left me high and dry this morning." Hands propped on her hips, the expression on her face could only be called "Irate Woman." Little Miss Julie had missed her calling as an actress. "It's gonna take more than lunch to get back in my good graces, and you *know* what I mean."

"Whatever you say, baby." He forced the most contrite expression he could muster without busting out laughing and shrugged at Travers.

The red-faced deputy slowly backed toward the door, obviously dismayed to find nothing more than a lover's quarrel. "You sure, Bon?"

"I've got him right where I want him, Dan." Her eyes softened, and her mouth curved into a serene smile that made Wynn shiver.

17

I stood at the door giving Dan a little finger wave and thinking what a phenomenal dumbass he was. I also had the not-so-small matter of Wynn to deal with and my job, which I in no way felt like doing.

I was tired. Not lack-of-sleep tired, but the mental kind that ground you down under its heel.

"So what now?" he asked from behind me.

I let the door slide closed and sagged against it. "I'm supposed to go to work, and don't even think I'm going to apologize to you."

"I know this has been hard for you." He eased closer, his hands outstretched in a nonthreatening manner that might appeal to a Rottweiler.

"I'm not a rabid dog; I'm an angry woman."

"Why don't we take a day off?"

"Can we really afford a day off?"

"I suppose not," he glumly admitted. They had only a week left.

"Besides, Tony and I have to do make-ready on 8-A. I'm still mad at you."

"I know." He wrapped his arms around me, making me feel secure even though logic dictated he was the last person I should feel safe with. "I'm sorry. Why don't you let me go through your stuff—"

"No way. Not without me here. Why don't you go cook or something?"

Yeah, it was mean, talking to Wynn like that. But I just wanted him out of my apartment and away from me for a while. I wanted a chance to catch my breath.

I slacked through the day, doing as little painting as possible. I talked Tony into closing up early and was in the middle of faking my way through some yard work when a red sedan pulled into the visitor's parking lot and a stranger climbed out.

He wasn't the type of man you could miss, and not just because most men in Cielo didn't wear suits unless they were going to a funeral or a wedding—both of which meant a trip to church.

This man was going to neither.

The expensive suit, coupled with the power tie and lavender shirt, was rather arresting, as was his height and broad shoulders. Something about him reminded me of Wynn, except colder. Much colder, calmer, more put together. The way he walked, like he owned the planet and everyone on it. Thin-lipped, almost grim, as he climbed the stairs and knocked on the door of Wynn's apartment.

A shiver worked its way down my spine. He was trouble in the worst way. Trouble I didn't need.

I pulled the brim of my ball cap lower over my eyes and waved to Tara, who was lounging at the pool. No amount of Wynn's good cooking or great sex could ease the sense of foreboding that nibbled at me from the inside out. I felt sick to my stomach, and I wanted to hide, but there was no hiding from him. He was the kind of man who'd find you no matter what. No matter where you ran, no matter where you hid.

"You okay, Bonnie?" Tara slipped her sunglasses off her nose, concern filling her deep brown eyes.

The taste of fear was so thick in my throat I couldn't speak, so I just shrugged. The sound of my name coming from the balcony mere seconds after the man disappeared into Wynn's place nearly sent me out of my skin. I made Wynn call me a second time before I finally turned around on feet heavy with dread.

He motioned for me to join him, and judging from the look on his face, he wasn't any happier than I was about our visitor.

I pointed to my wrist, opting for the first excuse I could think of. "I'm still on the clock."

The stranger appeared behind Wynn, and it was all I could do to read his lips, "That her?"

I glanced at Tara again, taking assurance in her presence and the sound of music blaring from JoJo's office. There were too many witnesses for him to kill me.

Yet.

18

Wynn led John back inside, still trying to adjust to his brother's arrival and, more important, figure out why he'd come.

"Wynn, what the fuck do you think you're doing?" Even sitting on the flower couch from hell, John still looked as unruffled and put together as he probably had this morning when he'd gotten on that plane in Florida. His suit was unwrinkled, his shirt still immaculate, his tie still in snug against his neck.

Six years older than Wynn, John had always been a bit larger than life, until they were adults anyway. Now Wynn knew he was just a cold-blooded, unfeeling bastard, incapable of lying or of having a normal relationship. Which explained why he was probably Dad's favorite, despite a very short stint as an FBI agent that he'd never bothered to explain. John's one and only attempt to escape his destiny.

It wasn't right to dislike family; it wasn't normal to be afraid of your family, but if there was one person Wynn didn't want to cross, it was John. Dani was the only one capable of going head-to-head with John, just like she did their dad. "I'm doing exactly what Dad told me."

"She knows who you are and now she knows who I am. Wynn, you know what that means?"

"It means shit! If you hadn't come here, she wouldn't know who you were. I didn't tell you to come here. You've only got yourself to blame for that. And if you have a problem with how I'm running things, go home!" He collapsed in the chair under the window, conscious of the sound of his neighbor's television being turned down.

No more yelling. He couldn't afford to raise the suspicions of his neighbors. He had enough trouble to deal with right here in front of him.

"I wouldn't have come if you hadn't made her sister disappear. You know what I have to do." His voice was as calm as if they were discussing whether to go out for ice cream after dinner or take in a movie.

Just like Wynn had mentioned, cold-blooded.

"You lay one hand on her and you'll answer to me."

"You're sleeping with her." He pulled his phone out of his jacket pocket and flipped it open.

"Put that away." Wynn leaned forward, elbows propped on his knees. He wouldn't allow John to call their dad. It'd be the end of him. It'd be the end of Julie, and he didn't want that either. In the worst way.

"Dad," John said, his phone programmed to recognize his voice and dial accordingly.

Wynn lunged, snatching the phone out of his brother's hand and racing for the kitchen. He hit the END button, hoping he'd cut it off before the call went through, then slipped the chip out of the back as John slammed into him. His brother had him in a headlock before he could react. His heart was pounding, trying to compensate for the sudden lack of oxygen as his fingers fumbled to get the chip down the disposal and flip the switch. He heard Julie's voice and the sound of running feet; then he could breathe. Julie and John hit the wall behind him so hard it vibrated. Something fell off his neighbor's wall and crashed to the ground.

Wynn lunged forward and flipped on the garbage disposal, conscious of the sound of breaking dishes and his brother's grunts behind him. While the disposal struggled to chew up the tiny card, Wynn sucked in a few deep breaths and turned to see how much damage had been done. John now had Julie backed against the kitchen wall, his forearm pressed against her throat. Wynn grabbed the collar of his brother's expensive dress shirt and wrenched him toward the far corner of the kitchen, then positioned himself between the two. "The last thing we need is another visit from the fucking cops. Now settle your shit down!"

John was doubled over in the corner, panting for breath, his narrow-eyed gaze on Wynn. "You really fucked this up, bro."

"Maybe so, maybe not, but I'm not letting you lay another hand on her."

"Or shoot me or drive me to Mexico and sell me to a brothel," Julie said from behind him. Her hands were gentle as she patted his back. "I'll shut the front door before anyone comes snooping."

"You okay?" He shifted forward to let her by, maintaining his position between her and John.

She was pale and moving slowly. Her hands shook a bit, but she managed a tiny smile. "I'm fine."

"Look at you!" John said.

Wynn felt a hand grab his shoulder, then he went reeling forward. The wall and his long arm span saved him from ending up on his face on the living room floor. Only his desire to avoid another run-in with the cops kept him from going after his brother. "You lay another hand on me and so help me God, I'll take *you* out to the desert and leave you there."

"You are totally pussed out! Some chick wraps her lips

around your dick and you're ready to commit hara-kiri on the family name." Unruffled quickly turned to anger as John's face reddened. "Do you realize what's at stake here, Wynn? Do you have any clue why Dad sent *you*?"

"Because he knew I'd have a problem with this job."

"*This job* has a name," Julie said, joining them in the kitchen.

"*This job* has the reputation of our entire family on the line," John said softly. "Dad guaranteed you'd deliver where two other men had failed. *You, Wynn*. No one else. And here you are fucking around with . . . her." He crossed his arms over his chest as if he could loom over her, intimidate her, even though he was actually a few inches shorter than Wynn.

"Want me to get your bat?" Wynn asked, pulling Julie against his side at the sound of her giggling.

Her small show of spunk filled him with a degree of pride nearly equal to the degree of protectiveness he felt toward her. God help him if he ever had to choose between the two of them, because it'd be a tough call.

"Now listen up!" Wynn took a step forward, cutting off John's view of Julie, and jabbed him in the chest. "It's not *my* fault the family's rep is on the line. I'm not the one who swore this job would be done. We're not fucking Wally World, and we don't give fucking money-back guarantees, John!"

"But you took the job."

"I had no choice." He raked his fingers through his hair. "Dad shoved it at me. I told him and I'll tell you, this job goes against everything I believe in. You might not have a code you live by, but I do."

"Code? You live by a code? You're a professional muscle, Wynn."

"I don't hurt normal people."

"I don't know whether to be insulted or not." Julie snorted.

She held her hands up in surrender. "I've had enough for one day. I'm going home."

"I'm sorry about dinner," Wynn said. Hopefully she knew he was sorry for more than just dinner.

"It's okay." She gave him a smile that eased the constriction he hadn't even realized gripped his chest. "I'll grab something."

Once she was gone, he went after John again. Wynn grabbed two fresh plates from the cabinet and handed one to his brother. "Now, what do you know that I don't?" He filled one plate with meatloaf and roasted sweet potatoes, then collapsed at the table. "Help yourself."

"You're such a puss." John filled his own plate, dusted the remains of broken dishes from the second chair, and sat.

"I'm a puss who's feeding you," he said around a bite of meatloaf. "And I don't hear you complaining about the food."

"Better than the airplane."

"Talk."

"I'm eating." He motioned to his plate with his fork, as if he were actually indignant.

"Fuck. Eat, then, but don't think you're not going to talk when you're done. *And* clean up the mess you made." He nodded toward the broken dishes and glasses on the floor.

"You made it," he said, pointing his fork at Wynn.

"No, you did, when you showed up here unannounced." In more ways than one.

19

I paced my apartment a while, occasionally rubbing my throat, which was tender and probably slightly bruised. I hadn't looked, though. I was afraid of what I'd see.

Why was John here? And what did his presence mean? Had someone raised the stakes? Put a price on my head, or Karen's and Kevin's? If the fight was any indication, Wynn wasn't happy to see him either, which meant nothing good could come of him being here.

Clyde sat on the back of the couch, his head slowly swaying back and forth every time I changed directions until he finally collapsed in a heap and rolled on his back. I sat beside him, slowly rubbing his belly, digging my fingers in his fur. His fur was soft and almost reassuring under my fingers as I sat there debating whether or not to run again.

Fighting Wynn was one thing, but fighting a killer was a whole other matter, and even to myself I wouldn't confess the terror I'd felt when John had pinned me against the kitchen wall. My sense of self-preservation insisted that John was exactly what Wynn had said he was. I hung my head, scrubbing my scalp and growling in frustration over the entire mess.

When the knock finally came at the door, I expected to see Wynn standing on the other side, not Tara, holding a half-empty bottle of Jack Daniel's Black Label.

She took advantage of my shock and pushed her way in, heading straight for the kitchen and riffling through cabinets until she found two leftover cups from the Speedie-Mart where Brad parked his truck. Speaking of which, he'd be at Darcy's tonight. I'd just have to take a pass.

"So who's the suit?" She rejoined me in the living room, sitting on the couch beside Clyde.

She poured the amber liquid in both glasses until they were a third of the way full. Clyde stretched and rolled his head back, exposing his neck for her to scratch.

"He's not someone you want to mess with, Tara." I sighed, joining her on the couch.

"Even I'm not dumb enough to mess with that, honey." She nudged a glass toward me.

"Sorry." I accepted it and swallowed a huge mouthful, wincing when the whiskey hit my empty stomach like a train on fire.

"You know, most of us are here for a reason."

"I know." I totally caught her drift. I wasn't the only one in hiding.

"I killed my ex-old man . . ."

I sagged against the cushions, the cup clutched in my hands. "Do I want to hear this?"

She studied me for a minute, all seriouslike, then shrugged. "Of course you do. He was some big-time drug dealer, or at least he *thought* he was. He hit me. I didn't like being hit, so he didn't do it too many times before I shoved a knife between his ribs."

"Ever hear of self-defense—"

"I was nineteen, and besides, I took ten grand. Even that ass-hole had a boss, and drug dealers don't like it when you steal from them."

"Don't you miss your family?" I asked, eyeing Clyde.

A cat and some photographs were all I had left of my family.

"Foster care." She gave me a cheeky smile. "Now, the suit . . ."

I didn't feel comfortable enough to tell her everything. I didn't feel comfortable telling *anyone* everything. I barely even trusted Wynn, and more than anything, I really just wanted all of this to be over, even though "over" didn't necessarily equate with any kind of a resolution or future. I chose to keep it simple. "He's a very bad man."

"And the new guy? The one you've been spending time with?"

"Brother," I said. "Why the hell are you here, Tara?"

"I saw your face earlier when he came steaming through the complex like a fucking freight train. You were scared shitless, girl." She sipped at her whiskey and pulled Clyde into her lap.

Funny how he only protested being held when it was me. I could even hear his motor running.

"If something happens to me, would you take him?"

"The cat? Sure. But nothing's gonna happen to you, Bonnie. We need you."

After Tara left, I paced a little longer, until I couldn't stand being trapped inside anymore and went for a walk. The sun hadn't quite set, and there was a breeze kicking up hard enough to stir dust and leave your mouth tasting like the desert. There was no movement from Wynn's apartment, just lamplight from the living room window. No shadows moved around, and I tried to imagine what the two brothers were talking about, or planning.

From the apartment below him came the sound of yelling

and glass breaking. A minute later, Tan came storming out *again*, Kaylee hot on his heels, tossing CDs and DVDs in his wake. One bounced off his back and hit the pavement with a clatter. I stood partially hidden by the bushes, watching them for a few more minutes. After Tan was gone, Kaylee and Maria stood in the doorway, arms wrapped around each other, worried expressions on both of their faces.

I debated whether to go see if they were okay when a voice from behind me caught my attention. "Nothing but trouble."

"Huh?"

Old Homer stood in his doorway, shaking his bald head. He was dressed in a white T-shirt, gray workpants, and black suspenders, his face clean-shaven, even this late in the day. "Young folks are nothing but trouble these days. Lots of goings-on lately."

"There sure has been." Smiling, I walked a little closer. How much had an old man who everyone, myself included, dismissed seen? Or heard? What else did he know?

"You keeping yourself out of trouble?" He gave me a toothy smile that seemed to hint at the fact he knew I hadn't been.

"Of course. Do I look like the trouble type to you?"

With a chuckle and a wave of his hand, he stepped back into his apartment and closed the door behind him.

Guess I was trouble.

I walked the complex a little longer, surprised at how calm everything seemed. Even over at Darcy's. Unable to resist the temptation, I peeked in the kitchen window for old time's sake. She and Brad were watching a movie. It was almost boring. With nothing to do and nowhere to go, I took a long hot shower and finished off the last of the whiskey Tara had left behind.

* * *

Wynn came knocking about three in the morning, his fingers beating a tattoo on the bedroom window until I finally woke up enough to push my hair off my face and peek through the blinds.

"Let me in," he mouthed.

I sat up, swinging my legs off the bed, and headed for the front door, tripping over Clyde along the way. He hissed and took off, scurrying for his favorite hiding place in my closet.

"You alone?" He was barefoot, dressed in sweats and a rumpled T-shirt, his hair all standing on end like he'd just gotten out of bed—which he had.

"No, I've got Brad, the super-mechanic, here." I swung the door open and waved him in.

"Very funny," he said, stepping inside.

Even though it was still early, I crossed to the kitchen and flipped the switch on the coffeepot, totally unprepared for the feel of Wynn pressed against me.

His hands slid up my bare arms, leaving goose bumps in their wake, and squeezed my shoulders. "Everything's going to be okay."

"Can I get some sort of money-back guarantee?"

"I promise."

"Pardon me if I'm not feeling reassured." I turned around, wanting to see his face when I asked him what I was going to ask him. "Why is John here?"

He sighed, his head sagging so I couldn't see his eyes before he met my gaze again. "He's afraid I won't finish the job."

"What exactly does 'finish the job' mean?" My fingers tightened on the edge of the counter.

"He means"—he reached under my T-shirt, his hands skimming the edge of my panties—"that I won't finish the job. Nothing more"—his hands slid higher, to my waist—"nothing less."

"How can you think about *that* at a time like this?" I sighed, my belly tightening ever so slightly and a tingling starting between my legs.

"I missed you." He grinned sheepishly.

It was difficult to tell in the dim light, but if I didn't know any better, I'd swear he was blushing. I'll admit, my knees felt the tiniest bit weak. I was flattered and couldn't resist a smile.

20

She was practically smirking at him. Wynn bit back a laugh.

He really had missed sleeping with her. He'd lain awake for hours, tossing and turning and listening to the sound of John snoring from his made-up bed on the living room couch.

Wynn needed the reassurance of being here almost as much as he needed to reassure her that everything was going to be okay. He'd worried all evening that she'd take off, but even she must have realized how futile that would have been.

"I thought you would have been here sooner. Matter of fact, when someone came knocking earlier, I thought it *was* you."

"So Brad really did come by." He grinned, knowing she was just yanking his chain.

"No, Tara. You could have knocked me over with a feather when I saw her standing on my doorstep."

"Tara?" His hands stopped their wandering. They did *not* need anyone else getting involved.

"Yeah. She was at the pool when John showed up. I was just killing time. Wynn, what are we going to do about John? I know he's your brother, but he makes me nervous as hell."

"Relax. I'll keep a rein on him." One way or another.

"Why didn't you rent a room under a fake name? Or did you?" Her eyes narrowed slightly with the last question.

"A serious miscalculation on my part. I gave JoJo my real first name because I'd already given *you* my real name." He grinned, earlier thoughts of a good snuggle with his girl nowhere near forgotten. "Don't worry about John. If Dad finds out he's here, he's in even bigger trouble than I am if I fuck up this job."

"What exactly happens if you fail?" She turned and retrieved two cups from the cupboard.

He wasn't in any mood for coffee or for talk about John and his dad. He wanted to spend what was left of the night with Julie.

He took the mugs from her and set them on the counter, then let his hands slide up the inside of her shirt again to cup her breasts. Her nipples hardened to tiny pebbles under his fingers, and his own body responded, blood pooling in his groin and swelling his cock.

"I can't believe you woke me up for this." Her sleepy-eyed grin made him chuckle.

"I'm a pig at heart."

"No, you're not," she replied. She shrugged out of his embrace and led him to the bedroom. Not that he took a whole lot of leading.

He dove for the bed, sliding under her down comforter.

"Impatient much," she teased, wiggling out of her sleep shirt.

The bed was still a bit warm and smelled like her, like vanilla with just a touch of lemon.

He ran his hands along the length of her. Smooth skin covering muscle developed from manual labor, her body still lush with rounded hips and full breasts.

She wriggled away, diving under the covers, her warm breath tickling his skin. She fondled his balls, gently rolling them between her fingers; her tongue was soft as it expertly caressed his cock. The previous day's tension ebbed away, and he relaxed against the pillows, moaning to himself just about the time Julie popped up like a jack-in-the-box.

"Besides, Brad was over at Darcy's tonight."

Laughing, he grabbed her waist, positioning her over his cock. "Oh yeah?"

"Yeah." She slid downward, the walls of her pussy milking him.

"You miss it?" He gasped, feeling himself grow harder.

"Not as much as I'm gonna miss this."

They lay curled up afterward, Julie's head cradled on his chest, listening to the world outside come to life. Doors slammed, a baby cried, the smell of bacon frying somewhere teased Wynn's nose and made his stomach growl.

"I'm scared," she muttered.

He pulled her tighter against him, his hand gently massaging her shoulder. "So am I, babe."

She pushed away from him, struggling to sit up. "I can't believe I have to go to work with all this shit going on. What are your plans for the day?"

"See if I can't convince John to get the hell out of Dodge, preferably today. And cook you dinner. Your choice," he coaxed.

"How 'bout we just grill some steaks. Something easy." She pulled fresh panties and a bra out of the dresser drawer and slid into them while she talked.

He got dressed and reheated the coffee, pressing a cup into her hand before he kissed her good-bye. "See ya for dinner."

"Yeah," she mumbled, her eyes focused on the kitchen floor, her head obviously a million miles away.

He walked the upstairs perimeter slowly, taking a look around as he did. The entire complex was quiet, like the calm before the storm. The storm being John, who chose that moment to step outside, dressed in a pair of pajama bottoms, his hair flopping over his forehead.

"Get back in there," he hissed, pointing at the front door. No way could John hear him from this distance.

John raised his right hand from behind his back and revealed a gun, silencer affixed. Wynn quickened his pace, rounding the last corner at a jog, the sting of his feet slapping against damp concrete and hot coffee sloshing on his hand minor inconveniences to the one his brother was about to cause.

"What the fuck are you doing?" he demanded, shoving John back inside and slamming the door behind them. "What the fuck are you thinking waving your *fucking* gun around like fucking Michael Corleone? You trying to scare the little kids down there or the old man? Does Dad know you've taken up smoking crack? Jesus H. Christ!"

"You know I don't do drugs." His serious expression prevented Wynn from knowing if he was joking or not.

"How can you be so calm?" He gave his brother another hard nudge in the shoulder, wincing when hot coffee splashed on his hand.

"It's my job to be calm." John sank down on the couch, the gun cradled in his lap like a favorite pet.

Jesus! Wynn ran his hand through his hair and blew out a heavy breath, then sank down in the chair and said just as calmly, "What the hell were you doing walking around out there with a loaded gun?"

"Habit." He shrugged nonchalantly.

Wynn shook his head, wishing he had something stronger than coffee to drink. "You *need* to *leave.*"

"Not till this job is done."

"This isn't *your* job, John. It's mine, and I'm going to finish it without *you.*"

"No, you're not." John gave him an arrogant smirk. "You're too wrapped up in that woman to see straight. You can't finish this job without me, because you can't see past your dick."

"You mean like I couldn't do the last job without you?" he asked, referring to Garrofolo's toe. "That went well."

"You have a tendency to puss out."

"You have a tendency to shoot first and ask questions later. You're a troublemaker, John. Furthermore, you're trouble I don't need right now. Why don't you go back to Florida and try to find Lisa?"

"Yeah, let's talk about that. Why the fuck did you call her?"

"I didn't." Now it was Wynn's turn to smirk.

"You are helping the enemy, Wynn."

"They're not *the enemy*! I'm being paid to get information from them. Nothing more. Nothing less. This isn't Afghanistan, John! This is the real world and Bonnie—*Julie*—has already lost her sister and her life. I'm not taking anything else away from her. I'm going to find the information, and I'm going to help her start over somewhere else. And you"—he jabbed a finger in his brother's direction—"are going to stay the fuck out of my way. Do you understand me?"

"Fine. Whatever you say, but I'm not leaving."

Wynn felt like grabbing his brother's gun off the table and shooting the smirk off his face. "I need you to get off my ass, John!"

"Okay."

"And stay out of my way."

"Fine!"

"Fine."

135

21

I watched the brothers, trying to figure out what was going on. What they'd been fighting about while they carried in bags of groceries from John's rental car. "Everything okay?"

"Everything's fine," Wynn said, coming over to give me a hug.

"That's very sweet," John said, breezing past us.

"Jealous?"

"Far from it, honey. I'm here to make sure you don't get my brother killed or, worse, disowned."

"Well, maybe you should stop being a dick and help us, then, asshole."

"You eat with that mouth?"

"And kiss your brother with it too! You eat with those hands?" I countered, referring to how he made his living.

He pokered up, his lips turning thin, and at the memory of last night's fight, I was afraid. I swallowed the lump of fear in my throat, thinking it was easy to see what made him so good at his job. He was a cold-hearted bastard. But I'd scored one for the home team.

I gave him my sweetest smile. "I have to get back to work."

"So do I," John said.

"Leaving so soon," I threw the comment over my shoulder as I turned the corner.

"Not hardly," John said, following me.

Wynn was hard on his heels.

I pasted a sneer on my face and spun around, ending up right in his face, ready to bluff him into thinking he was a tiny little blip on the radar of my life, that I had no fear of him. "Then why don't you make yourself useful, and go find my sister!"

He pulled back, his eyes narrowed. "Don't push me, woman."

"Woman? What? I won't like you when you're angry." Common sense dictated I shut the hell up and stop letting him know how much he'd gotten to me, but damn, it was hard.

From behind me came the sound of Tara snickering. "Don't let him get you all het up, Bonnie."

"You are some piece of work, lady. I've killed men for less."

"I bet you have."

"That's enough!" Wynn stepped between us, pushing John back a step or two while he gave me a warning look. "This isn't accomplishing anything. John, get those steaks upstairs while I set up the grill. Julie, go get cleaned up for dinner."

I cringed the minute my real name came out of his mouth, knowing Tara, who'd followed me, begging for an update, had heard. With a sigh, I turned toward her. She made a lip-zipping motion with her hand and gave me a reassuring smile. "Thanks, Tara."

"Maybe I can help," she offered.

"No!" Wynn insisted. "We're not dragging anyone else into this."

"Why not?" I countered, looking pointedly at John.

"Julie," Wynn warned with a shake of his head.

"She already knows a little bit." From the corner of my eye, I spotted JoJo bearing down on us, and I was in no mood for a confrontation with her after the night I'd had.

"How much did you tell her?"

"Not much."

JoJo was getting closer, and the last thing I wanted was a reprimand for my two days of slacking.

"Tara, how's your kitchen sink?" I asked.

To give her credit, Tara was quick on her feet. "Bad. Real bad. And you promised to fix it today."

"Later, guys." I followed Tara inside her apartment and closed the door behind me, shutting out Wynn and John and JoJo. "Your sink's not really clogged up, is it?"

"No way. I just said that." She sat on the couch with her legs crisscrossed, and I followed suit, choosing a bent cane rocker. She leaned forward, eyes wide, and whispered, "Has he really killed people?"

I didn't have the balls to actually say it, so I nodded instead. "And he's not going anywhere anytime soon."

"That's not good!"

"No, not at all. He says he won't leave until Wynn finishes the job."

"What exactly is the job?"

"To find something. Something small that I apparently brought from Arizona with me, but we've checked everything and we can't find it."

"Does the cat have a collar?" she asked.

"I checked it. Nothing."

"How well did you know your sister?"

"Apparently, *not* very well."

We both chuckled; then she continued, "If you were your sister, where would you have hidden it?"

Karen was a doctor. Which made her a problem-solver, though

not necessarily a creative one. "If it was in the envelope with the photos, then it's long gone. Other than that or the cat's collar, I have no fucking clue."

We chatted a bit longer and she promised to think on it.

"I better get." I opened the door and stepped into the late-afternoon heat, my mind going in at least fifty different directions.

Tony was over closing up 8-A for the day. Wynn and John were upstairs doing God knows what to some steaks and each other. JoJo's Cadillac was gone, her day of beggaring the boss with her online purchases over. Jeanette was in the pool with her kids again.

I leaned against the gate, my arms propped on the top bar, my chin propped on my arms, watching them and letting the sun bake my skin through my work shirt. Joey was seven, and Angel was almost nine. Jeanette was quiet, kept to herself, and kept a keen eye on her kids. She never dated, never socialized, didn't even go to church. Not that skipping church made her a bad person, but church and the bar were the two highlights of life in Cielo. She worked part-time for a local insurance agent while Darcy babysat. She lived frugally, though there wasn't much above frugal in Cielo.

I'd never thought much about her, beyond the few facts I knew, but after hearing about Tara, I found myself wondering where she'd come from and what had brought her here.

A door slammed behind me. I turned and looked up at the second floor, tracking John as he came down the stairs and joined me.

"Kill Wynn yet?"

My quip didn't even get a chuckle. More like a harrumph . . . or something. "He's marinating the steaks."

"You know, if you'd smile, you'd look like him." If anything, his lips thinned. I scooted away just the tiniest bit.

"Who's that?" he asked, nodding toward the pool.

140

"Jeanette. She lives here." *Duh, Julie.*

He rubbed his jaw, stood with me a few minutes longer, and then turned and went back upstairs as Mrs. Hollis's son opened the gate and joined Jeanette in the pool. He was thin but no one would ever call him scrawny; the legs sticking out of his oversized swimsuit were a far cry from the toothpicks you might imagine.

Around sundown, he'd take off on his BMX bike and not come back until nearly midnight. What the hell he found to get into around here at night I didn't even want to know. His pale skin was a testament to spending too much time inside, in his room, probably surfing porn sites and eating Doritos and maybe lifting weights. I guess what his mother didn't know suited her just fine.

Uncomfortable would be a nice way of describing dinner with Wynn and John. After a dozen or more covert looks between the two brothers, I finally threw my fork across my half-eaten steak and sat back, arms crossed, pinning both men to their chairs with my best no-bullshit look. "What's going on?"

"Nothing," Wynn said with an easy smile. "Now finish your dinner. I slaved all day over that."

"I don't suppose you figured out a solution to our little dilemma?"

They both shook their heads.

"Are you leaving soon?" I asked, turning my attention to John.

This time they both gave each other that look again.

"I'm not sure," John said.

"Well, what are you sure of?"

"Your neighbor—"

"Shut up, John!" Wynn stood and grabbed the tea pitcher off the counter, refilling all our glasses.

"What's the story on that girl Tara?" John finally asked between bites of his baked potato.

"Don't know. But I bet I can get you a date with her, if you're nice."

"What about that woman at the pool?"

"Jeanette? She's a single mom." I didn't like his questions at all. I didn't like where this was going, even if I had no clue.

"The old man across the way? The big guy coming out of the downstairs apartment early this morning?" he asked, referring to Brad.

"I. Don't. Know. I've made it my business to stay the hell out of other people's business, if you know what I mean." I gave him a pointed look.

A look he returned in kind.

"That's not what I heard. Wynn says you know everything about everyone around here. Says you make the people around here your business." He steepled his fingers and rested his chin on them.

"Did you—"

"No!" Wynn finally sat back down, his face a suspicious shade of red.

"Relax, hotshot. I know that woman from somewhere. The one at the pool." He sounded so calm, so sure.

I almost wanted to run downstairs and tell Jeanette to pack her bags, load up her kids, and get the hell out of Cielo. Because if someone like *him* knew someone like *her*, it wasn't going to end well.

22

"You scared her," Wynn said after he'd reluctantly let Julie leave. John didn't respond. "You'll be lucky if she doesn't tell that poor woman."

"Don't be naive." John sat with his feet propped on the coffee table, tapping at the keys on his laptop.

"Did you get any more information from Dad?"

"Didn't hear from him today. Didn't contact him either. Don't want him to know I'm here. Remember?"

"The clock is ticking, and we've got to find that information, John. If you're not gonna help, then fucking leave already."

Finally, his brother looked up at him. *Good, he had his attention.*

"Not my job. My job is clean-up. My job involves long distances and great aim. Did you search her apartment?" John asked, referring to Julie.

Wynn caught the verbal jab about distance and chose to ignore it. "Yeah, we did that the first night—"

"*You*. Not *we*. How do you know she's not hiding something?"

"I know."

"Because you're banging her? That's fantastic, Wynn."

"Don't hold it against me that you're an asexual bastard who'd rather jack off than have a real relationship."

John didn't date, hadn't had a steady girlfriend in years, and Mom had long lamented the fact that he would be the last to give her any grandchildren—if he did at all. Women were a means to an end where he was concerned.

"I'd rather jack off than fuck my client's quarry."

"I hate to break it to you, but that's because you're not human."

"I have some things to do." Red-faced, he lurched to his feet, grabbed his keys off the table, and slammed out of the apartment, leaving Wynn alone.

With a quiet chuckle, Wynn headed to Julie's, hoping he could calm her down.

23

I'd spent the day avoiding Wynn and in turn, John, tired of sparring with him, tired of not knowing what we were looking for.

And just flat-out tired.

I'd even skipped dinner with Wynn, a ritual I'd come to love over the last couple of weeks, in favor of a Lean Cuisine, which had left me cranky and unsatisfied.

Hands in my pockets, I walked the few short blocks to the convenience store, kicking up dirt with the toes of my shoes as I went. Hopefully, a sugar fix would settle me down, or something.

There was more traffic than usual, and after two police cars and a sedan went whizzing past me, I turned, trying to gauge what I had missed. They were too far away now, their license plate lost in a swirl of dust. I didn't hear sirens, their lights hadn't been flashing, but in my gut I knew something wasn't right.

Stretching my legs had turned into an exercise in frustration. I couldn't relax. I couldn't unwind. Inside the store, I wandered the aisles, using the selection of candy as an almost ritualistic way to calm myself when two men came inside.

Men like them, like John, just didn't come to a place like Cielo, Texas, without bringing trouble along for the ride. They were dressed in suits, but not custom-made like John's, their shiny shoes covered with a coat of dust, both of them sporting aviator sunglasses and a little extra bulk under their jackets. They could have almost been twins with their matching haircuts and twinkie suits.

They spent a few minutes chatting with Frank up at the counter, then headed my way. I snatched up a bag of Skittles, prepared to step around them, but they were too quick. They had me trapped in the aisle between them.

I knew what they were even before they spoke. Hell, I'd known when they hit the door. Some things you just didn't need spelled out for you.

"I'm Agent Ross and this is Agent Montgomery," the shorter one said as he handed me a card.

"How's it going?" I took the card, running my finger over the embossed logo of the FBI before shoving it in my pocket. No, I had no inclination to pour all my woes out to these two, not when I was in possession of more than a few fake IDs, a wad of cash, and two missing sisters. "You here on vacation?"

"No," Agent Ross said.

"We're looking for this woman." Agent Montgomery pulled a photo out of jacket pocket and shoved it in my face.

It was Jeanette, younger, blonder, less worn-down-looking, a smile on her face as she crossed a street in some unknown city.

"Doesn't ring a bell, sorry."

"We got a tip she was here in Cielo. At the apartment complex Frank says you work at."

"So why aren't you out doing surveillance or whatever?" I

moved a little farther down the rack and picked up an oversized Snickers bar, angling to get around them. I didn't ask what they wanted her for. I didn't care, hoping that if I gave them very little information, they'd leave town as quickly as they'd come. And if my suspicions were right, their presence was all due to a phone call from Johnny boy.

"We are." That was Montgomery. I had a feeling he was the mean one, the one who'd play bad cop. He had thin lips and wore a perpetual frown.

Not so twinlike, I know.

"If you have any contact with her," Ross said, "please call us."

Yeah. Right. Stay tuned, guys. "Will do." I headed for the counter, paid, and stepped outside where a dark blue sedan was parked.

I walked around the driver's side, glancing at the trunk on my way by. It had a rental-car sticker on the corner. I didn't know enough about the FBI to know if they were legit or if they ever rented cars, but anyone could fake a business card and a badge.

I took my time getting back to the complex, waiting to see if they'd pass me, then circling back to the resident's parking lot.

The goons were sitting across the street under the oak tree. One of them toasted me with a soda can and being ballsier than the average dumbass, I walked over and tapped on the window.

Ross rolled it down and slipped his sunglasses off his nose. "Think of something?"

"Yeah"—I held out the Snickers—"thought you might need this."

Trouble had come to Cielo.

Going to Wynn's in a complete female frenzy was out of the question, as was heading for Jeanette's, so I did the next best thing and headed for Tara's, rapping furiously on her front door.

When she answered, I pulled the card from my pocket and shoved it in her face. "Look legit to you?"

"I guess." She shrugged and took it from me, motioning for me to come in. "Did you hear Tan left Kaylee?"

"Yeah, she's sleeping with his sister."

Her face twisted into something between a laugh and a grimace, and we got a case of the giggles together. "Poor guy." She glanced at my hand, which was still holding the card. "So where'd you get that?"

"I ran into some FBI agents at the Speedie-Mart."

"Are they looking for your friend, John?" she asked, smirking.

I smirked back. "Unfortunately, *no*. They were looking for Jeanette!"

"Porter?" She leaned forward, eyes wide.

"Porter," I said, nodding.

"No freakin' way!"

"Yes freakin' way! I need you to go tell her while I sneak up to Wynn's, 'cause the last thing I need is for the Feds to get a whiff of 'eau de thug.' "

She giggled and bounced on the couch some, like I'd just asked her to go skinny-dipping with me. "What are you gonna do?"

"I dunno," I said, twisting the doorknob. "We'll figure it out. You know what? Just . . . Just bring her to Wynn's."

The last thing any of us needed was more attention, especially Federal attention. For that matter, I couldn't imagine what poor Jeanette had done to even *warrant* Federal attention. I should have asked, but then, that would have been admitting I knew her.

I took the stairs two at a time, hoping like hell Ross and Montgomery weren't skulking around behind the sign, waiting to see where I'd go.

I never even knocked, hoping if they were watching, they'd think I lived here.

John was sitting on the couch, dressed in a pair of pajama bottoms with red polka dots, fondling—er, cleaning—his gun.

"That's very attractive, Johnny." I closed the door behind me, doing my best not to out and out laugh. Despite the gun, the scars, and washboard abs, he looked, in a word, ridiculous. "Get dressed."

"You sure are awful bossy." He leaned forward and gently set the gun on the coffee table.

"Wynn, get out here. We've got trouble." I directed my attention back to John. "Now get dressed before our company arrives."

With a scowl, John disappeared into the bathroom as Wynn joined me. The front door opened and Tara and Jeanette joined us.

"Say hello to Jeanette Porter, Wynn." I waved a hand in her direction.

"I'm going back downstairs to stay with the kids," Tara said.

Jeanette hesitated at the doorstep, and once again I found myself wondering what in the hell some FBI agents wanted with someone like her. "Tara said you wanted to see me."

John rejoined us, the expression on his face closed and wary, his stance firm.

"Did you call them, John?" I asked, letting the anger that had been simmering boil over.

"Call who?" Wynn took a seat, confusion on his face.

"What's this about?" Jeanette tightened the tie holding her robe closed and edged closer to me.

"Get that mean-ass look off your face, John," I ordered, pointing to the couch, "and sit your ass down. You're scaring her."

He took the spot he'd been sitting in earlier, right in front of his gun.

"*You're* scaring *me*," Wynn countered.

"Guess who I ran into at the Speedie-Mart? Guess who they were looking for?" I gave John a pointed look, knowing good and well he'd called them for no reason that I could think of except to cause trouble.

"Honey," Wynn said, "I have no idea who you're talking about."

"The FBI."

"Oh my God," Jeanette muttered, leaning into me. "The kids."

I wrapped an arm around her waist. I felt for her. I felt a kinship with her, remembering my own fear when Wynn had first showed up. "They're parked across the road, so you can't run. Not yet."

"Why the hell did you call them, John?" Wynn was white-knuckling the chair's arms. "You know I don't need this shit right now. What the fuck were you thinking?"

"I think the better question is, why do they want her?" John leveled his narrow-eyed gaze on her.

"What does it matter? Does Jeanette look like a stone-cold killer to you? Or maybe a drug dealer? Does she look like someone who needs to be picked up by the Feds? And what happens to her kids if she's arrested, you cold-hearted piece of shit?" I tightened my grip on Jeanette, wanting nothing more than to walk over and kick the hell out of John.

"John, how could you be so stupid? So *fucking* stupid! You're not even supposed to be here, and you call your feebie friends!"

"Friends?!" A shot full of adrenaline raced through me, narrowing my vision and leaving me weak-kneed.

"John here used to be a Fed." Wynn hooked a thumb in his brother's direction, then made a shushing motion. "Very hush-hush stuff. You know, the kind they deny."

Jeanette was now crying softly. "I did what I thought—"

"I don't even want to know." Wynn held up a hand to stop her from talking. "The less we know the better."

"He's right," I said. We gave each other a look of understanding and agreement. "We have to get her out of here."

"You have to turn her over to the Feds." John glared at me, but it didn't work.

I wasn't buying it. "You're an asshole, and now you're going to help us get her out of here."

"No."

"Yes. You. Are!" I matched him evil look for evil look.

"Yes, you are," Wynn said calmly. Calm enough to even make me shiver, and he was the last person I'd ever be scared of. "Now start talking."

"She's wanted in—"

"John! The facts!"

He glared at me for a few heartbeats before answering. "Okay, fine, I called, but she's—"

"And you made fun of me for having a whacked-out code." Wynn muttered a few more choice cuss words under his breath. "What's their next move?"

"They'll probably come at daybreak," he said, leaning into the cushions in obvious defeat. "Nothing heavy-duty. Just the two of them before she's up and gone for the day."

I would have laughed if the matter hadn't been so serious. If I hadn't been so tired and angry. "So we've got all night to get her and the kids out of here."

John corrected me with a slight shake of his head. "You do."

"*We* do," I corrected, crossing my arms over my chest. "You're gonna take your gun, tuck it into the back of your pants, walk her down to her apartment, and stand guard while she packs. Jeanette, do you have money?"

She nodded and wiped the tears from her face. "I've got a stash, yeah."

I was nowhere near done with big brother. "John, how much do you have?"

"I'm not giving her any money."

"The hell you're not," Wynn said. "I know for a fact you always carry a couple grand on you. Now cough it up."

"Give me one good reason why I should."

Jesus, he was gonna give me an ulcer! "Because if you don't, I'm going to march my happy ass across the street and tell those FBI agents you're a hit man and you've been stalking me."

With an angry look at all three of us, John got up and disappeared. I could hear him rummaging around in Wynn's bedroom.

"I've got a couple grand stashed away too," Wynn said, standing up.

"I don't know—" Jeanette started.

I interrupted her. "You don't have any choice."

"They've already seen you," Wynn said, nodding in my direction, "so you need to stay put. Tara can take Jeanette in her car, and I can take the kids in mine. We can meet up in Alpine, and then Tara can ride back with me."

John returned and threw two rubber-banded stacks of what appeared to be hundred-dollar bills on the coffee table. "Happy now?"

"Very, you fucking scrooge."

Wynn eased to his feet, smoothing his jeans down his legs,

and picked up the money. "And if you ever do anything like this again, I'll take you out and kill you myself. Understand me, big brother?"

I spent two very tense hours pacing my apartment and waiting on Tara and Wynn's return. I'd left John on his own, figuring he was sleeping the sleep of the righteous or something asinine like that. Finally, the doorknob turned and I ran for it, throwing my arms around Wynn's neck. "Did everything go okay?"

"Everything went fine. They'll be long gone before the agents realize what happened, but we have another problem," he said, smoothing my hair off my face.

"What now?"

Shivering at the early morning chill he'd brought in with him, I turned and crossed to the couch, curling my feet up underneath me.

"The Feds know who you are. It probably won't be long before they figure out your identity is fake, and I don't doubt they're going to know you helped Jeanette."

I sank deeper into the couch as if I could ward off this latest catastrophe. "Oh my God, Wynn, what do we do?"

"We get you out of here. Back to Dallas. I really do have a place there, and we get you a new identity."

"I have identities," I said, brightening. At least I could do something. "I have two."

"Good. Get packing. I'll wake up John. We need to leave as soon as possible."

"Are they still out there?" I asked, referring to the agents who were parked across the road earlier.

"They're gone—for now." His eyebrows rose sharply. "How fast can you pack?"

"Fifteen minutes, but what about Tara?"

"We can't take Tara with us, honey." He sighed.

"I know, but can I at least say good-bye?"

He nodded, as if he understood that I needed to say good-bye to *someone*. I needed to feel like someone might miss me when I was gone.

Once he'd left, I loaded a sleepy, angry Clyde into his carrier and locked him up tight, then set about gathering up photographs, which I *was* taking with me; clothes; cash; and the fake identities I'd squirreled away in the Sheetrock of my bedroom closet. I looked at the gaping three-inch hole I'd left, knowing if the Feds found it, the game was up.

Oh well, I'd be long gone before they did.

Wynn came and got my bags. I turned out all the lights and grabbed the handle on the cat carrier, ready to head out after I stopped at Tony's and then Tara's. Tony was sleepy, but he caught on quick. He knew I was in trouble and leaving. Tara was wide awake and waiting for me when I knocked a few minutes later.

"Wynn told me on the way back." She swung the door open and let me into the darkened apartment. Only the light from the bathroom in the hall illuminated the room. "The Feds."

"Huh?" I set the carrier down.

"I left the lights off in case they came back."

This was all my fault. If I hadn't wanted to help Jeanette, I wouldn't be running again, but there was no way I was going to let her get picked up. I didn't care why the Feds wanted her; I'd do it again.

My throat thick with tears, I hugged her. In my three years on the run, she was the closest I'd come to having a friend. And even though she'd driven me nuts plenty of times with her sexual antics and a multitude of boyfriends, I'd still admired her free spirit.

She shoved something into my jeans pocket. "E-mail me, okay? When you get settled somewhere."

"Maybe you can come visit," I said, even though we both knew it would probably never happen. I swiped at my own face and picked up the cat carrier, thankful Clyde was being so quiet. "Take care of yourself."

"You too. And don't forget to write!"

24

John left ahead of them, riding point and keeping an eye out for the Feds. Wynn was still mad and unsure if he'd ever forgive his brother for the shit he'd just pulled. His brother's uncharacteristic lack of common sense had left him reeling.

What the hell had he been thinking?

Wynn loaded up the last of Julie's bags and slammed the trunk, then helped her get Clyde settled in the backseat. "Get in back with him; stay low until we get out of town. I don't want anyone knowing you're back there."

With a nod, she pushed the carrier over and slid in. Wynn closed the door behind her and circled around to the driver's side, worried at how quiet she'd been. Taking her to his place in Dallas was the latest in a list of bad ideas, and once his dad found out how terribly wrong things had gone, there'd be hell to pay. He'd worry about that later.

He backed out of his spot, pulled into the street, and headed through town for Alpine. "We should be in Dallas by late morning," he whispered.

He eased past streets still asleep, closed stores, the occasional pickup truck, already regretting his decision to take Julie away from what had to have been a security blanket for her. What had been her only security since leaving Scottsdale three years before.

"I'm scared," came a tiny voice from the backseat. It didn't even sound like the same Julie.

Guilt dug at him. It'd take her a while to get her bearings back.

"Everything's going to be fine," he said, as much to reassure her as himself. He'd said that same thing to her more times in the last couple weeks than he could count. "Just fine."

"I'm holding you to that," she said with a sniffle.

They stopped in Alpine so Julie could get in the front seat while John went in the store for some Cokes.

"Why don't you go to Midland and catch a plane home?" Wynn suggested.

"Can't." John blew on his coffee, glancing at where Julie sat, the windows up, her fingers wrapped around her soda.

"You need to leave before this gets any more fucked up than it is."

John shook his head. "Mom and Dad know where I've been. If I go home, they'll want a report, and you know I can't lie." John could disseminate maybe but lie, never. He got busted every time.

"And besides, Mom already knows I'm here with you."

Even better yet. No wonder he hadn't heard from her since the furniture arrived.

"What does Mom know?"

"Just that I'm here."

"That's fabulous, John, thanks. Anything else you'd like to do to fuck up my life?" Wynn dug his keys out of his pocket, ready to get back on the road and away from his brother before he did something stupid, like hit him.

"That's it."

That was enough.

Julie slept most of the drive, waking up in time to see the mid-morning sun bounce off the Dallas skyscrapers. She gave him a sleepy smile, peeked over the backseat at Clyde, and stretched.

"He's been awful quiet back there."

"Cars traumatize him into a mushy puddle of 'fraidy cat," she muttered, clearing her voice. "Where exactly are we going?"

"We're here. Just a few more minutes north."

"What about John?"

"He's behind us." He caught the unhappy look on her face. "Listen, I don't like it anymore than you do, but we've got to keep him with us until this is over."

"We should have brought Tara to distract him."

Chuckling, Wynn reached over and took her hand, giving it a nice squeeze. At least here, in Dallas, there were fewer unknowns for him to deal with, but like Julie, he almost wished Tara was with them too.

At this time of the morning, I-75 was a breeze, not like it'd be late in the evening with rush-hour traffic. In no time at all, they pulled into Wynn's driveway, the garage door sliding open ahead of them. His BMW was parked in one stall, and there was just enough room for the Blazer. He'd ditch it as soon as he could, just in case anyone back in Cielo connected the two of them and gave the Feds a description of his truck. Better yet, he'd let John take care of it since this mess was pretty much his fault.

He pulled to a stop just short of the garage and helped Julie

159

get all her stuff out, pressing the house key into her hand. "Wait on the porch until I get there to disengage the alarm."

She chuckled, a low rusty sound caused from stress and lack of sleep. "I can't think of the last time I walked into a house and had to think about things like alarms."

Once he had Julie settled in his bedroom, Wynn let Clyde out and ran to the store for food, cat litter, and a litter box. He came through the back door, his arms full of bags, to find John sitting at the kitchen table, doing his best to ignore Danielle, who sat across from him yakking his ear off. She was dressed in a causal but expensive yellow tracksuit, her pale blond hair pulled up haphazardly on top of her head.

"There's more out in the car." Wynn set the bags on the countertop, wondering what was on John's mind or if Dani had just talked him numb. He crossed the kitchen and pressed a kiss to her cheek. "What are you doing here?"

She gave him a smirk, then put her fingers to her ear, imitating a phone. "Yo, Dani, gonna be gone a while. Get my mail. Love ya."

For the first time in a long time, his older brother actually looked ruffled, but then, driving all night could do that to you. "That woman Jeanette was wanted for kidnapping."

"What woman?" Dani asked. "What's going on? John, what did you do?"

"And you know this because?" Wynn asked, ignoring Dani for now.

"Because her fucking picture is on the FBI Web site!" John stood up and headed out the back door for the rest of the groceries, slamming it behind him.

While he waited for his brother's return, Wynn unloaded the bags, stashing milk in the fridge and meat in the freezer.

"Wynnie," Dani coaxed, "what's going on? John's never this quiet. And he said something about you getting involved with a woman, a what do you call it? A job? Do you think it's safe, getting involved with her?"

He fixed up the litter box for Clyde while he talked. "I care about her. A lot. She's . . . a good person. She put herself at risk to help someone else. Hell, she took me down with a bat." He grinned to himself at the memory.

"Sounds like a real trooper."

"I think you'll like her."

"When do I get to meet her?" Dani asked.

"Soon as she wakes up." He ripped open the bag of cat food, and Clyde magically appeared on the countertop. "Hey, boy. You know if Dad finds out you're in the middle of this . . ."

"I'll tell him it's John's fault."

"I heard that, runt." John set the last five bags on the counter. "Just because Jeanette was a wanted woman doesn't make her a bad person."

"She was wanted for kidnapping her kids." John started unloading them, slamming canned goods on the countertop.

"*Her* kids, John. *Her kids!* And just in case you didn't get the memo, things aren't always black and white. It's not like she kills people for a living, and you're not an FBI agent anymore."

"And I haven't been for a long time."

"You're supposed to stay under their radar. Under *everybody's* radar."

"She was wanted for kidnapping. You and your code," John spat. "*I don't hurt real people.* Whatever. You think that makes you a saint or something?"

Now was not the time to pick a fight with his brother, but John, of all people, should know that. Wynn scrubbed at his face, fatigue settling into his bones. "No, hell no. But whatever fucked-up code *you* live by has put us all in jeopardy, John."

"Your little girlfriend did when she decided to help that woman."

"John," Dani scolded, "that's just wrong."

"You know if those Feds follow us, and we end up having to go underground, Dad'll be pissed."

"What if Julie didn't bring whatever we're looking for? Did you think about that, ace?" He turned around to face John, who was studying Clyde.

"Oh, I think she brought it."

25

Embarassed at sleeping most of the day away, I reluctantly rolled out from between the silky soft sheets of Wynn's bed, hoping a shower would clear the last of the fog from my head. The bathroom, like the rest of the house, was a soothing combination of old and new, with black and white check tile on the walls and floors, a pedestal sink with antique faucets and five, count them, five shower heads in the oversized stall. Believe me, I enjoyed every one of them, before I finally forced myself out of the shower and wrapped myself in a fluffy, oversized towel.

The bedroom was a soothing moss green, with white crown moldings and refinished wood floors. An oriental rug muffled the sound of my footsteps as I crossed to my bag and dug out some clean clothes and my toiletries. Once I gathered my hair in a ponytail and brushed my teeth, I set out to find Wynn . . . and John.

From the hall, I could see the kitchen, a few more doors, and an arched doorway. It opened onto a living room painted a pale, muted green that coordinated with his bedroom. The furniture was expensive but not fancy: a beige couch and matching chair with boldly patterned throw pillows, a flat-screen television, another oriental rug. I crossed to the picture window, drawn in by the sight of a tree in Wynn's front yard with huge white blossoms on it. The yard was perfectly manicured, and all the houses that I could see appeared just as nice and as old as Wynn's.

"Wynn's got chicken on the grill."

I spun around in shock, a shot of adrenaline coursing through me, causing my fingertips to tingle. Other than the clock ticking quietly on the mantel, I hadn't heard a thing. How John had managed to stay so quiet on these hardwood floors was anyone's guess, but I suppose that was his job. "Thanks."

"Get some rest?" he asked, turning toward the kitchen.

"Yeah." I followed. My head was fuzzy as I tried to absorb the events of the last forty-eight hours.

We had only a few days left, and we were still no closer to finding what Sunset Pharmaceuticals was after than we had been when we started. "How's Clyde?"

"Seems fine," John said, pointing to the kitchen counter.

Clyde was sprawled out on the cool granite countertop, only inches from a bowl of food. Something spicy-smelling was cooking on the stove, and my stomach rumbled, reminding me of how long it had been since I'd eaten.

"Wynn's gonna regret letting him get up there."

John harrumphed and silently led the way outside, where Wynn stood at the grill, flipping chicken breasts and sipping a Corona. A slender blonde in a stylish tracksuit sat at the table.

"There's beer in the fridge." She gave me a friendly smile, the type that said, "I'm totally not threatened by you." "And since my brothers are too rude to introduce me, I'm Danielle."

"Thanks, but no beer for me. I think I need to wake up first." I shook her hand and settled in a padded lawn chair.

Feet curled under me, I listened to the sound of cars, the faint beep of someone blowing their horn, and studied what looked suspiciously like smog on the horizon. Somewhere nearby a garage door slid up, or closed, squealing slightly in its tracks.

A siren wailed.

The sounds of humanity, of hustle and bustle and a big city. Excitement warred with fear over what my future held. I had to hang on to every penny, so a shopping spree at Neiman's was out, but I couldn't resist a smile at the thought.

"What are you smiling about?" John asked from the chair beside me.

"You wouldn't understand."

Wynn chuckled, as if he knew exactly why I'd been smiling, and Danielle giggled.

I curled up a little tighter in the chair and just enjoyed watching Wynn work for a while, wondering when Danielle had shown up. Wynn had napped beside me for a while. The dent in his pillow confirmed it, but I'd been so tired I'd barely moved when he slipped out of bed. After driving all night, he must be bushed. "You get some rest?"

"Yeah."

"If you two are done cooing, we need to talk."

"I wasn't cooing," I said, shifting to face John so I could scowl at him. "I don't coo."

"Yes, you do."

"No—"

"John, quit being a bully," Danielle said.

"John has a theory." Wynn interrupted me before John and I could end up in World War Three.

"About?"

John gave me an enigmatic smile that sent shivers down my back. "Clyde."

26

"What about Clyde?" Julie's voice sounded thin and strained, as if John was the last person she wanted focusing on Clyde.

"Hear him out." Wynn set down the tongs he'd been flipping chicken with and walked over to squeeze her shoulder.

He got Julie a beer from the minifridge he kept on the back porch, twisted off the top, and handed it to her.

"I think it's in the cat," John said.

"Actually"—Dani raised her fingers, wiggling them in the air—"it was my idea."

"What's in the cat? The . . . thing?" Julie glanced at Danielle, a worried expression on her face.

"I know everything," Danielle said. "Anyway, last year my cat got lost."

John sipped his beer, the expression on his face serious, contemplative. "After she found him, the vet put a chip in his neck in case he ever got lost again. Karen said you had the evidence with you. You've checked everywhere *but* the cat. Logic dictates, it's in Clyde."

The idea had merit but . . . "I still don't understand how the hell we're going to find out if there's a chip or whatever in the cat."

"We cut him open." John grinned at both women, as if he was pleased with himself for coming up with such an ingenious idea. If he hadn't been so far away, Wynn would have smacked him upside the head.

"Ew, John! You so need therapy." Danielle tossed a chip at him, and it bounced off his chest.

"Don't even think about killing my cat, asshole." Julie set her beer down and crossed her arms over her chest. "Do you really think it's in Clyde?"

"That's a fucked-up name for a cat, by the way." John snorted.

"Thank you for your unsolicited opinion, asshole."

"Whoa!" Wynn held out both hands. "Please don't start, you two. And, Dani, no more throwing food. We've all had a long couple of days. Let's just take it easy, okay? We can't kill the cat." Wynn sighed. As much as Julie hated that cat, there was no way she'd let them, and there was no way Wynn would have any part of anything like that. "We'll have to find a vet to do an X-ray or something. At this point, I'm game for anything."

"Oh. My. God." A wide-eyed Danielle glanced at each of them. "Do y'all watch *X Files*?"

Wynn pressed his lips together to keep from laughing at his sister. Julie and John both denied any direct or current knowledge of *X Files*.

"Okay." Danielle's arms were flapping so much she almost knocked the beer from Wynn's hand. "There was this one episode in season two or three, *might* have been four, I can't remember which. But anyway, Scully, she's this FBI agent—"

"Get to the point," John barked.

Danielle sighed in frustration and rolled her eyes in Julie's direction. "I'm telling the story, John, now quit interrupting! They took this alien chip out of Scully's neck! Then she goes to the grocery store—"

That was all it took, and Wynn was doubled over with laughter. Even John broke into a rusty chuckle. Finally, Wynn recovered, took a deep breath, and wiped his eyes, grinning at Julie who'd spilled a bit of beer on the front of her shirt.

"What?" Danielle looked at all three of them in obvious confusion. "She did!"

"She went to the store after they took a chip out of her neck." Julie snickered and sipped her beer, her green eyes twinkling.

"Yeah! But eventually they had to put it back in because Scully got—"

"Dani." John barked a warning, his lips twitching.

"I'm not sure I want to." Danielle crossed her arms over her chest, waiting until they were all finally calm.

"*Please,* continue," Wynn said. With Danielle, you definitely got more flies with honey.

"She scanned the chip and the cash register went nuts!" One last arm wave sent her bottle of beer flying. It clattered to the deck, spewing foam everywhere. "I'm so sorry, Wynnie."

"It's okay. I'll hose it off tomorrow," he reassured her, leaning over to pick it up.

"What exactly are you planning?" Julie countered, her shoulders shaking, her face scrunched up while she tried to talk around the laughter about to spill over. "You gonna sneak Clyde into the grocery store and scan him?"

Danielle was bouncing again. "That's a great idea. We can go late at night and—"

"We're not sneaking the cat into the store. We'll just call a vet first thing tomorrow and get him X-rayed."

"I'll call Dr. Burnside." Danielle leaned over and dug a cell phone from her purse.

"Maybe a vet we don't know would be better." Wynn stood and crossed to the chicken, giving it one last flip and peeling open the foil containing vegetables that were steaming.

"Don't be silly." She stood up and trotted inside, closing the door behind her.

From where he stood, Wynn could see her at the counter, talking and waving her hand, stopping every once in a while to pet Clyde, who'd joined her.

"Doc said bring him in at eight tomorrow morning." She was practically bubbling over when she rejoined them. "So I'll just get here around seven-thirty."

"You're not going," John said.

"Don't be silly. Of course I'm going."

"He's right." Wynn set the platter of chicken and roasted vegetables on the table. "You can't go."

"No, he's not, and yes, I can." Dani stood up and got herself a fresh beer.

"Oh, let her go," Julie said. "Can I help? With dinner."

"There's plates and stuff on the counter and some beans warming on the stove."

While Julie went to get them, Wynn did his best to convince Danielle not to get any more involved. "We appreciate your help, sis, really, but it's a bad idea for you to get any more involved than you already are."

"Well, if I'm already involved, a little more shouldn't matter."

"Dani, you can't help."

"Why can't she?" Julie set the plates on the table and handed out silverware.

"Because," she huffed, cocking her hip to one side, "Dad doesn't like me to be involved in the family business." She sat down and stabbed at a chicken breast with a fork, putting it on her plate, then turned her attention to Julie. "Do you know how hard it is to bring home boyfriends when your brothers and dad are thugs?"

"I resent that," John said.

"The last time the family got together to meet my boyfriend was after he threatened to leave me if I didn't take him home to meet the folks. We'd been dating eight months. John here shows up toting his gun, and he and Daddy took Rog, my boyfriend, out shooting. I got dumped a week later."

"At least they brought him back," Julie said with a snicker.

Danielle, being Danielle, joined in. Before too long, both girls were laughing too hard to eat. Even John managed to crack a smile.

"I can just imagine what the family arguments were like."

"Lord, honey, try to imagine being grounded! Try to imagine how scared my prom date was after Dad finished showing him his Cuban cigar collection."

"Oh, you poor baby."

"Lay off, John." Wynn frowned at his brother, in no mood for another fight.

"And I thought having sisters was tough."

Despite all of Wynn's pleading, Danielle was at his house at 7:30. The fact that she'd gotten up so early, dressed to the nines in designer slacks and a matching blouse, her long hair caught in a casual updo, her makeup in place, *and* managed to get to his house *on time* was, in a word, shocking. Dani wasn't exactly known for her promptness, but she was so loveable no one cared.

"Morning, Wynnie."

"If you call me that again, I'll let John shoot you." Only his mom was allowed to call him Wynnie, and only because he couldn't make her stop. He shoved the coffeepot onto the warming plate.

"I heard that." John joined them in the kitchen, already dressed in perfectly creased khaki pants and a perfectly pressed white polo shirt.

"Where's Julie?"

"She's coming," Wynn said.

"You know, I've been thinking . . ." Dani gave them her sweetest smile.

Wynn tensed up in preparation for whatever harebrained notion was getting ready to come out of her mouth.

"I'm scared." John picked up Clyde, who'd been happily munching away on kitty kibble, and shoved him in his carrier.

"Very funny. Why are you even here?" Dani demanded.

"Because Dad hasn't called me about any jobs, and if I go home—"

"He'll get the truth out of you about calling the Feds. Dork," Dani finished with a smile. "Anyway, I was thinking that maybe just Julie and I should go."

"No way," John said.

Dani leaned in closer and took a good hard look at John, then circled the counter and patted him down. "You're taking your gun to the vet?"

"Is there anything he doesn't do with that gun?" Julie asked, breezing into the kitchen. The dark circles under her eyes were nearly gone, and she actually looked rested, dressed in her usual jeans and T-shirt.

"I don't even want to know the answer to that," Dani said.

"You know why they don't want us to go," John said, giving Wynn a deadpan look he couldn't interpret.

His gut tightened, a sure sign he wasn't going to like the answer and, more important, neither would Dani. "Huh?"

"They wanna scan the cat. See if he makes the cash register go nuts."

"Actually"—Dani grinned, her eyes lighting up—"we were planning on sneaking him into Target and just using one of the scanners in the store."

27

While Dani and John bickered, I fixed myself a cup of coffee for the road and picked up Clyde's cat carrier. He hissed at me, but his weight settled in the back, a sure sign of his unhappiness. Two car trips in two days was a lot. Poor guy. Even he didn't deserve treatment like this.

"What do we tell the vet?" I asked Wynn, who'd followed us outside.

"Oh, don't worry, honey." Dani swept past, patting my arm as she went. "We'll just make it up as we go." She clicked the alarm on her Mustang and opened the passenger door, pushing the seat forward so I could put Clyde in.

I stopped and gave Wynn an I-don't-know-about-this look. As crazy as Dani and John's idea was about the evidence being *in* Clyde, it did make sense.

Karen was a doctor; she could have done something like that. I sure as hell wish she'd been a bit more specific when she'd told Lisa what we were looking for, though.

"I still say we just slice him open."

"Shut up, John," Dani and I chorused as we slid into the car.

* * *

We sped down the street, turned a couple times, and headed down Mockingbird Lane, crossing the highway, which was wall to wall cars. I couldn't remember the last time I'd seen that much traffic.

"How exactly did you get involved with my brother?"

My stomach clenched, but Dani didn't give me a chance to work up a response before she'd started talking again. I got the feeling that happened a lot with her.

"I know you're a job, but my brothers don't usually bring their work home with them, if you know what I mean." She flashed me a quick grin, then turned her attention back to the road.

"I'm a job, all right." I sighed. "If there's a chip or something in Clyde, it could have the information that Wynn's been searching for. And if he finds it, then my sister and brother-in-law are safe."

"Where are they?"

"I have no clue. They disappeared three years ago, and up until Wynn showed up, I thought they were dead." While she drove, I filled her in on the rest of the story. She peppered me with questions, and she was thorough, which meant leaving anything out was impossible. "You should have gone into the family business."

"Don't even joke about that." She eased to a stop at a red light and slipped her sunglasses down her nose, giving me a serious expression.

"I didn't mean you'd . . ." I left it just hanging there between us, unable to even finish the sentence. To say the words.

Dani had no problem finishing it for me. "Kill people? I know. But I have issues with the family business and, more important, my father's cavalier attitude about the family business."

"I can imagine," I said, remembering Wynn's story about how Dani donated money to charity in her father's name.

"I just want to be an English teacher." She sighed. "To be honest, I'm surprised Wynn's still in it. I figured he would have gotten out a long time ago."

"What do you think he would have done if not . . . what he does now?"

"Wynn could have been anything." Her gentle, easy smile said how much she thought of him. "A teacher, a lawyer, anything."

"He said he was a disappointment to his father, but you know, that's a tough occupation to expect your children to follow you into."

"He expected all his boys to follow in his footsteps, and me to marry and spit out babies. I might have gone into law, but then he'd have been forced to disown me." She gave me another look, one I couldn't interpret, and turned into a low-slung brick building. "I guess you and Wynn are pretty close."

"Yeah." Pretty close seemed like a mild way to put it.

"What are your intentions toward my brother?" She gave me a pointed look, one fine eyebrow arched.

More than anything, I wished I could return her grin, but as much as it hurt to think about, my time with Wynn was almost over. "I don't think your brother and I have any kind of a future."

"Hmmpf. I guess we'll just have to see about that. As soon as we get old Clyde back there taken care of."

Clyde meowed when he heard his name, a pitiful sound that announced his frustration to the world—or at least to Dani and me.

"Let's get this over with, and then maybe we can run by PetSmart and get Clyde some treaties." Dani unhooked her seat

177

belt and slipped out from behind the wheel, then ducked her head back inside. "Come on. Let's go!"

Carting Clyde, I followed her inside and took a seat while she checked us in. He started growling the first time he heard a muffled dog bark, and from the sound of it, there were plenty of them locked up somewhere we couldn't see.

Luckily, we were first and didn't have long to wait before a veterinary assistant escorted us into a tiny room. At her instruction, I took Clyde out so she could weigh him.

"Pet's name?"

"Clyde."

She never blinked. I could only imagine she'd heard worse. "Last name."

"He doesn't have a last name," I said, glancing at Dani and trying not to laugh.

"What's your last name?"

I stared at her for two long heartbeats, then said, "James. Clyde James."

"And what exactly are we seeing Mr. James for?"

She was so not cute! "We're trying to find out if he has a chip in him."

"A microchip?" she clarified with a smile.

"Yeah. We weren't sure if he needed an X-ray or what," I explained, shooting a quick, guilty glance in Dani's direction.

"Oh no, we have a special scanner. I'll be right back." She left the room, returning a minute or two later with a handheld scanner, similar to the hand scanners at the grocery store. "Hold him down, please."

While I kept a firm grip on his sides, she ran the scanner over his body, coming back to his neck, her cheerful expression turning into a frown. "It's registering something, but it's not an identification chip."

"Maybe we should have taken him to the grocery store," Dani said with a giggle.

I snorted, nearly losing my grip on Clyde.

"Let me go get the doctor," she said, ignoring Dani's joke.

This time our wait was longer, and I was forced to let Clyde go. He prowled the room, his hackles raised, sniffing at everything and backing into a corner when the door opened again.

"Morning, Dani," Dr. Burnside said as he slipped a pair of half glasses onto the bridge of his nose. "What do we have here?"

I picked Clyde up as the assistant explained the problem. Nodding thoughtfully, the doc waved the scanner over Clyde's neck again and came to the same conclusion. "There's something in there all right. Let's do a quick X-ray and—"

"Can you take it out?" I asked. Whatever was in Clyde's neck obviously shouldn't be there.

"Are you sure that's what you want?" The doc's eyebrows crinkled in concern, his fingers gently kneading the scruff of Clyde's neck.

"We're sure." Dani vigorously nodded her head.

"All right, then. You two wait outside, and we'll get this guy fixed up in no time."

I followed Dani out, stopping at the doorway to ask the vet one more question. "Can we see it, after you take it out?"

"If you'd like, sure. I have to admit, I'm a bit curious myself as to why someone would put a chip in your cat." He smiled, shrugging slightly bent shoulders.

Nodding slowly, I said, "You and me both."

Ten minutes later, we were out of there, Clyde in his carrier and a chip the size of a crumb tucked safely in my purse.

"Do you know what's on it?" Dani asked as we sped back to Wynn's.

"No clue. Something about forging tests on some drug. I don't even know what kind of drug."

"You mean like *lying to the FDA*?"

"Yeah. Exactly like lying to the FDA." Because Kevin's bosses had lied to the FDA, I'd lost him, both my sisters, my livelihood, and my home just so some greedy assholes could turn a profit. "Bastards."

"Do you want to know what's on that chip?"

It wasn't just about the chip. If I blindly turned the chip over to Wynn, I'd never know why Karen and Kevin were forced to run away—other than the aforementioned lies, of course. Whether I turned it over or not, I ran the risk of never actually having a life again. In other words, I had nothing to lose. "Yes. I want to know."

Dani slipped the Mustang into the right lane and shot onto the freeway. The car settled between an Escalade and a Lexus, and we cruised along at a slow pace in bumper-to-bumper traffic.

The farther we got from Wynn's, the more I worried they'd worry and come looking for us. "Where exactly are we going?"

"To see a man about a chip."

Fifteen minutes later, we were still in Dallas but about as far from the refined neighborhood Wynn lived in as possible. The area was old, with narrow streets and businesses jammed between converted warehouses, all of it tucked away in the shadow of the city's high-rises.

"Interesting. Where the hell are we?"

"Welcome to Deep Ellum." She parked the car outside an older brick building jammed up between a bunch of others. "Don't forget Clyde."

I got the cat and followed her, stepping carefully across the cracked sidewalk to join her.

By the time I got there, she was already talking into the intercom. "It's me, baby, and I brought you something you're just going to *love.*"

A few minutes later, we heard footsteps, and the door opened, revealing an attractive, heavyset young man with supershort dark hair and wire-rimmed glasses.

I bit my lip, holding back a grin as they kissed, trying hard not to laugh as Dani introduced Eli as her boyfriend. "Has he met the family yet?"

"No, and I don't want to." Smiling, he offered his hand and we shook.

A glowing Dani clutched his free hand. "If it's high-tech, Eli here can figure it out."

Poor Eli's cheeks turned pink as he led us inside and up the stairs. His loft had a queen-sized bed tucked next to what passed for the kitchen. Every other available space was taken up with tables covered with computers and other electronic equipment I couldn't identify.

Eli took a seat at the longest table, located just under the windows, and held out his hand.

I pulled the glass tube containing the chip from my purse and passed it to Dani, who gave it to him. "We want the information off that chip."

"You sure there's actually something on it?" He held it up to the light, studying it.

Dani and I glanced at each other and shrugged simultaneously. "Pretty sure."

There was still the odd, and minuscule, chance that chip wasn't what we'd been looking for. But what else could it be?

"Okay then"—he smiled—"let me see what I can do."

"How . . . how long do you think it'll take?" I asked.

Clyde wasn't going to stand being stuck in that carrier for much longer, and I'd missed breakfast. Not to mention the guys would eventually wonder where we were. The clock was ticking.

"I'm honestly not sure. It depends on what I find once I figure out how to access any data that might be stored on it. Could be a couple hours, could be a couple days."

We didn't have a couple days; hell, we didn't have a couple of hours. "We can hold off John and Wynn for an hour or two, but days we don't have, Dani." I didn't particularly like lying to Wynn after he'd been so good to me, but I didn't see we had any other choice at this point. If he knew we'd dragged yet another person, let alone Dani's boyfriend, into this, he'd be furious, and rightly so.

"She's right, honey."

"Come back in an hour. Let me see what I can do."

Back downstairs, I suggested we call Wynn and lie, maybe go get a cup of coffee to kill some time until Eli got done working his high-tech voodoo.

Grinning from ear to ear, Dani pulled her cell phone from her purse. "We can take him to PetSmart, just like I told the guys we would. That way we're not lying, and he can get out and ride in the buggy."

Once she made the call, we were off again, heading back toward the highway and the nearest pet store. This time Dani took Clyde. She scooped him out of his carrier and marched him into the store, heading straight to the fish and rodents. I followed after, hurriedly grabbing a shopping cart.

"See the yummy treats, Clyde?"

He purred, lounging in her arms and lapping up every crumb of attention she threw his way.

I rolled my eyes at a passing sales clerk and nudged the cart in her direction. "I'm going to get him a collar."

"And a leash. He needs a leash. We're going to pick out some toys."

I spent ten minutes debating the merits of various collars and leashes and trying to find a matched set, then another five scolding myself for wasting time on a leash for a cat I'd probably have to give away when this was all over. Never mind that he'd probably never use it.

"Any luck?" Dani asked when she and Clyde joined me. She'd put him in a basket and covered him in half a dozen toys. He actually looked pretty comfy, lounging on a blue and green checked pet cushion, his demonic yellow eyes reminding me not to be fooled by his relaxed demeanor. He could decide to turn on us and go after those fish any minute now.

"Yeah." I held up the red collar and leash I'd chosen. "I doubt we'll get much mileage out of a leash with him, though."

"You never know. At the very least it's another play toy."

"What if the guys followed us and they know we went to Eli's?" I asked, dropping the leash on Clyde and teasing him with it.

He twisted around in the basket, determined to make it his slave, the action making it tougher for Dani to hang on to him.

"Let me take him." I held out my hand, slipping the basket on my arm, and we slowly walked to the front of the store to check out.

"I don't think they'd bother." She draped an arm over my shoulders. "Relax, worry wart."

Easy for her to say. It wasn't her ass on the line.

28

Wynn had spent the morning straightening up the house and cooking, more as a way to burn off nervous energy than anything else—and to avoid John, who seemed to run every time Wynn headed his way with the vacuum. At least when the girls called, he could finally relax. And relax he did, stretching out on the sofa for a quick nap until his cell phone rang. It wasn't Dani calling back, but his dad.

"I haven't had an update in days. Please tell me you're not leaving this until the last possible second."

"I'm not, sir."

"I want to talk with him when you're done," said his mother.

"You know better than to leave me hanging like this. Did you or did you not find the Lyons yet?"

"Not yet."

"Not yet? Not yet?" His dad's voice rose on the second question, a question that didn't really need an answer.

"I'm working a different angle. We're in the home stretch."

"We?" his father barked.

"Us. You and me? I'm just tying up some loose ends, Dad."

From his spot on the other side of the bar, John grinned. Too bad Wynn had nothing to throw at him. Shifting closer to the cat food, he covered the mouthpiece and whispered, "You want to talk to him?"

John shook his head, backing away from the counter.

"Then shut up."

"What did you just say?" his father demanded.

"Nothing, sir. I promise I'll have this wrapped up in time."

"You better. Here's your mother."

There was the sound of fumbling as he passed the phone off and then his mother's bright voice in his ear. "How's it going?"

"Everything's fine, Mom." He relaxed at the sound of her voice, the knot in his gut loosening just a bit.

"Just a minute, dear. Let me get outside."

He waited patiently until the back door had closed.

"Now," she gently huffed, "tell me what's really going on."

"Besides what John's told you?" He felt bad for scolding his mother, even slightly, but it had to be said. A sigh was the only sort of acknowledgment he got. "The Feds showed up, so we're in Dallas now."

"The Feds?" she breathed. "Why in the world . . ."

"John." Wynn grinned at his brother.

"They aren't after him again, are they?"

"No, he called them to turn in a woman who'd kidnapped her children, and Julie insisted we help the woman get away."

"So *she's* still with you?"

"She's out with Dani now, trying to find out if the evidence is in the cat. And please don't yell at me. Your daughter refused to go home and mind her own business."

"Oh, dear. Don't tell your father. You know how he gets about Danielle." The sound of a long drawn-out sigh, a sigh only a mother could give, filled Wynn's ear. "Now, that woman?"

"Mom, I've got it all under control."

John snorted, and Wynn picked up a piece of cat food and tossed it at him.

"Wynnie, honey—"

"Mom, *under control*. I—"

"I don't believe you. Your involvement with this woman is trouble in the worst way, honey. What do you think your father would do if he found out? The shit would hit the proverbial fan."

"That's why you sent John? Because you were afraid Dad would find out?"

"Technically, dear, I didn't send him. He elected to come on his own. What happens to this woman—"

"Her name is Julie."

"All right. What happens to *Julie* when this is all over? Have you even thought about that?"

"Yes—"

"I'm not just saying this because of your father. I'm truly worried about you, Wynn, and I don't want to see you get hurt."

"Nobody ever plans to get hurt, Mom. I'll be fine."

"You know you have to send her away when this is all over. It's for your own good, as well as hers."

"I know." As much as he didn't like it, she was right.

Once he got what Dad wanted from Julie, he'd put her on a plane to Brazil, just like they'd discussed.

29

Eli had found something.

We'd driven through Jack in the Box for a late breakfast and were headed back to his place when he called. My mouth watered the entire way. It'd been far too long since I'd had fast food—*good fast food*. Even Clyde thought so, if his howls from the backseat were any indication, but he'd have to settle for some canned cat food we'd picked up at the pet store.

Back at Eli's, we hustled upstairs, carrying the food and Clyde, who jumped onto the kitchen counter the minute he was free, pacing back and forth impatiently for his treat. It wasn't the same as real chicken, but he didn't complain.

"Do you love me?" Eli asked, accepting the monster-sized breakfast sandwich Dani handed him.

"You know I do. Now, what'd you find, sugar pie?"

"Sugar pie," I whispered, glancing at Clyde.

Eli, who was in the process of unwrapping his food, glanced at me, as if daring me to make fun of Dani's pet name for him. Frankly, I was too busy wondering what they were doing together. Not that Eli wasn't good-looking, and obviously he had a brain, but two different worlds was an understatement.

"So, what did you find?" I plucked at my own, much smaller sandwich, too anxious to eat, despite missing breakfast.

"Sunset Pharmaceuticals has been very bad and *very busy.*" He punctuated his sentence with the sandwich, waving it around, then taking a bite when he was done talking. We had to wait until he'd chewed and swallowed to get the rest of the story. "From what I read, they've falsified data on five different drugs, including one that's getting ready to hit the market."

Wynn's timely deadline now made sense, but five drugs was . . . I shook my head, trying to process it all. "Are you sure, Eli?"

"Yup." He motioned with his head to the printer located near the foot of the bed.

I scooped it up before Dani could, and a minor scuffle ensued as we fought over the paper. "I gave up my life for this," I finally insisted, giving an extra-firm tug. "And besides, the less you know the better."

"Fine." Dani threw up her hands and returned to her own breakfast, feeding Clyde tiny pieces of sausage.

By the time I was through reading, I was sick to my stomach. Giving Wynn the evidence hadn't sounded like such a bad trade-off when it was one drug, but Sunset had been perpetrating a fraud, *a huge fraud,* and making a mint in the process, for years.

And their fraud had lost me everything.

My mind in chaos, I washed and dried my hands, standing silently by while Dani finished reading. Giving them what they wanted and getting a free pass to a new life was all well and good when it was one drug. And yes, I knew it was a very gray area, the difference between one and five. And maybe it didn't make me a very good person, my willingness to trade my freedom so easily.

Jesus! I rubbed my temples, squeezing my scalp in frustration, then reached out to scratch Clyde, who rolled onto his back and knocked over an empty glass.

"Dani, this is bad." Bad was an understatement. No wonder Sunset had been so worried.

This was a catastrophe.

"What do you want to do?" she asked softly.

"You need to do *something*," Eli added between bites.

"I was willing to trade my life for one drug, to trade my family's lives, but not five. Someone needs to pay, Danielle."

She nodded slowly, reluctance written on her face. Making donations in your father's name was one thing; going against his direct orders was a whole other ball game. "Whatever you want me to do, I'll help."

"You can't get involved. But I will need you to lie . . . a little." The only way to protect Dani, Wynn, and yes, even John, was to keep them in the dark over what I was thinking of doing.

"What do you have in mind?"

"We weren't here. I never met Eli."

"It took longer at the vet's than we thought, time got away from us at PetSmart, and we stopped to eat." She shrugged her perky shoulders. Too bad all my problems couldn't be solved as easily.

"With the cat?" Eli's chair squeaked as he turned around.

"We could have sat in the car with Clyde."

"Sounds good." I nodded and scooped up the printouts. "I need another set of these. Better yet, make it two more."

With a nod, Eli turned back to his computer, clicking a few more buttons. The printer started to hum and spit out more papers. I motioned to Dani to stay put and crossed to where Eli sat. "Can you keep a secret from your girlfriend?" I asked softly.

He leaned back, glanced at her and smiled before catching my eye again. "Sure. But just this one time."

191

I reached for another stool, pulling it close to him and sitting down. "If you were going to send this information to someone, who would you choose? Someone big."

"Anderson Cooper? *Dateline*? *20/20*? *60 Minutes*?"

"Get me their addresses, please." I grabbed a piece of paper off the printer to sketch out a rough draft of my letter. "And the FDA too. Definitely the FDA."

"Jon Stewart," Dani added, letting me know she'd heard me. "Or the *National Enquirer*."

Eli and I smiled at each other, at her silliness, which was much needed at that point, before he went back to work.

"Laugh if you want, but they've broken some big stories in their day."

"I think *Dateline* and maybe *60 Minutes* will do. I need mailers and stamps," I said to Dani. "And I need to write a letter."

"The post office sells mailers." She gathered her purse and picked up the remains of our breakfast, tossing them in the garbage can except for some egg from my sandwich now clutched in Clyde's paws.

"Let him have it. He deserves it after everything we've put him through in the last couple of days."

After I typed up the letter on Eli's computer, I loaded Clyde, and his egg, into the carrier and locked it, then gathered up the printouts from Eli, including the addresses I needed, and headed downstairs while Dani said her good-byes. "Don't forget the chip!"

We stopped at the post office on the way back to Wynn's. It took me ten minutes tops to scribble names and addresses on the envelopes and mail them. I did it before I could think about what I was doing, about what I'd done. And, forgive the melodrama, before I could think about the consequences of my actions.

"Drive fast," I said once I was back in the car.

"We've been gone way too long. I'm surprised they haven't called."

I glanced in the side-view mirror, still not one hundred percent convinced that the guys, or at least John, hadn't followed us. Nothing looked suspicious, but I still felt uneasy. A feeling I'd just have to chalk up to nerves.

"So you're going to give Wynn the chip?" Dani asked as she took the exit for Wynn's house.

"Yeah. He doesn't need to know about the rest."

"Do you have money?" She knew I was planning on running, even if I hadn't said it.

That was not a question I could answer. The less she knew, the better. My attention remained on the passing scenery.

"Where will you go?" She downshifted and eased to a stop at a red light.

"I don't know." Brazil was out. That was the first place Wynn would look for me—if he looked for me. Or it'd be the first place someone else would look for me, after they forced the information out of Wynn.

A few minutes later, we pulled into Wynn's driveway, ready for showtime.

"We never went to Eli's," I said softly.

"I know, I know. PetSmart, Jack in the Box, and the vet's office, but it might be a tough sell. We've been gone a while."

"We'll wing it." I climbed out of the car, ready to reach for Clyde when Wynn came darting out the door and down the steps to the car.

"Where the hell have y'all been?" He ducked inside the car, getting Clyde.

I stuffed down the nerves threatening to strangle me and formed a response. "We ran some errands."

"Yeah," Dani added, "wait till you see the toys we got Clyde."

"You didn't answer your cell phone." John stood on the top of the steps, a scowl on his face.

"I don't have one." I gingerly maneuvered out of Wynn's way, praying he didn't look too closely at me.

"I meant her!" He pointed at Dani.

"I must have shut it off after I called you." She crossed to the back door, swinging the bags from PetSmart as she went.

"Well, what happened?" Wynn asked so softly I almost didn't hear him. So soft, in fact, I wondered if he really wanted to hear the answer.

"We got it. A chip in Clyde's neck." Which wasn't a lie. I reminded myself of that as I headed for the door, leaving him to follow with the cat.

He grabbed my arm, spinning me around, his eyes raking over me repeatedly as if he were looking for something. Was my guilt that obvious?

"Are you okay?"

"Yeah." I shrugged. "I guess. What do you want me to say, Wynn?" Once again, I'd be on the run, which would have been the case regardless. Except this time I knew my family was out there somewhere. Not that I had any clue where to find them, but I still had Lisa's friend's phone number, and Miami Beach would be my first stop. It was a place to start.

"I don't know. I was just worried about you."

From inside the crate, Clyde started to howl, as if he sensed his imminent freedom and refused to be held a second longer.

"We did it. It's over." I figure I had, at best, forty-eight hours before I had to get lost.

"We need to talk."

"Sure." I gently pulled my arm free of his grip. "Later. We'll talk later."

I turned and headed inside, unwilling to talk to him with John so close by. Afraid that one of them would look at me just a little too closely and know that something was up.

Once Clyde was free, he immediately disappeared, and so did Dani, claiming she had to get books for the new semester before they were all gone. "I'll let you guys deal with the chip from this point."

"This is fantastic." John leaned in closer, peering at the chip through the plastic bag. "We've got to call Dad back ASAP."

"Wait!" Wynn reached out, covering the baggie with his hand and cutting off John's view. "Just slow down a minute."

"Slow down? Little brother, there's no waiting about it. You finished the job; now call Dad and tell him it's done." He shook his head, a huge grin on his face. "I didn't think you'd pull this off, Wynn."

"I can't." He pulled the vial toward him.

I had visions of them fighting over it, the glass vial breaking and the chip flying off to land in the sink, lost in the drain forever, like something out of a black comedy.

"We don't even know what's on this chip."

"Jesus H. Christ, Wynn, who gives a shit!"

As much as I appreciated Wynn's twinge of conscience, I couldn't have him backing down now. Not when I'd already taken care of the problem. Besides, I had to play the game—to the end. I covered his hand with mine, squeezing his fingers. "Wynn, let them have it."

"They're about to commit fraud. What if someone dies and we knew?"

"The deal was the chip for my freedom. If you don't turn that chip in, I can't be free."

195

"We could work something out."

Wynn might have forgotten John's presence, but I hadn't. "There's nothing to work out."

"Listen to the lady." John stood there, practically smirking.

"That's what you want?" Wynn's Adam's apple bobbled up and down a bit.

It wasn't what I wanted, in the worst possible way. I wanted to stay with Wynn, I wanted my sisters back, I didn't want to give up Clyde, but I couldn't have it all. I took a deep breath and said as forcefully as possible, "It's what I want."

"Good." John whipped out his cell phone.

"Not so fast, tiger." I slapped the counter to get his attention. "I have to leave, remember? That's the deal, and I think I deserve a head start."

"So?"

"So, maybe, since your happy ass can't lie, you should take the chip to your dad while Wynn helps me get lost." And I could have one last night, alone, with him.

"I—"

"What if your dad asks where I went or what happened to me? Or he asks you about my sister? You'll be forced to tell him the truth, and I don't need him or, worse, Sunset, sending someone to do clean-up duty."

"She's right." Wynn slid the chip across the counter to John. "Take it. And go."

30

His face burning with anger and frustration, Wynn stood there, mentally willing his brother not to balk at finishing the job for him.

Especially after all the trouble he'd caused.

John looked at him and then at Julie before nodding and shoving the chip into his pocket. "Fine."

"You might want to be careful with that," Julie said, pointing at his jeans.

"It's been in a cat. How much more damage can I do?"

"I guess at this point, it doesn't matter." Julie chose that moment to turn three shades of white and sway on her feet.

Wynn caught her just before her knees gave out. "You okay?"

"I forgot to eat," she confessed, pressing the palm of her hand to her forehead, "and now I've got a raging headache."

"I thought y'all ate while you were out?" John asked.

Wynn was wondering the same thing.

"Forgive me if I was feeling a little off my feed. It's been a stressful couple of weeks, Johnny." The circles were back under her eyes, testifying to how tired, and probably frustrated, she was.

And maybe, just maybe, upset over leaving him.

John nodded, his eyes narrowed, and Wynn wondered what was on his mind. Sure the girls had taken their sweet time getting back, and sure Wynn had been worried, but he figured that was her way of saying good-bye to Clyde, and Dani, too, for that matter. Julie didn't want to leave any more than he wanted her to.

John, however, didn't look convinced. "Let me grab my stuff, and I'm outta here."

"Let's get you into bed and I'll make you some soup."

"I don't need you babying me, Wynn."

"It's my prerogative to baby you, if I want. And for that matter, this may be the last time I ever get to."

She nodded slowly, obviously reluctant to give in even a little. "Okay."

He got her tucked in and had a can of soup warming when John came out with his bags. "I'll call you when I get to Dad's."

"Thanks, and if I don't answer, leave a message." Wynn gave him a pointed look that said, "Don't sweat calling 'cause I probably won't answer."

True to his word, John was gone by the time Julie's soup was hot.

Wynn set the bowl on a tray with some crackers, hot tea, and a bottle of ibuprofen. Julie lay curled up in his bed, facing the far wall, and for a minute, he worried she might already be asleep. She turned her head at the sound of the floorboards creaking under his footsteps, giving him a weak smile and sitting up. He set the tray on her lap and went around to stretch out on his side of the bed.

"You look like you just lost your best friend."

She nodded hesitantly but refused to look at him, choosing to pick up the spoon instead. "You'll keep Clyde, won't you? Or give him to Dani? I think she'd . . ." Then she started to sniffle, and her eyes turned red, welling with tears. She set the tray on the floor and curled up with her backside pressed against him. "I don't know if I can do this, Wynn."

"We can figure something out, if you want to stay." He knew she'd say no, and she did. They both knew she had to get lost—just in case. He'd rather have her alive and gone than dead where he could visit her grave every day. "I'll call the air-line in the morning and get you a ticket to Brazil, and get you some cash."

"I've got cash."

"I want to make sure you're taken care of, at least for a little while. Now let me do this."

Her nod signaled that was that. He should have been worried at how easily she gave in, but he didn't want to dig too deeply, didn't want her to feel like she had to say things neither of them wanted to say. If he was smart, he'd go away, leave her alone, and let her cry.

"What about dinner?" he asked.

"I'm not very hungry."

"You will be later." He squeezed her side, snuggling closer, needing to remember how she smelled, how she felt, for later. "I'll fix anything you want."

"How about that chicken stuff you made the first night you cooked for me?"

"Anything else? Anything you want to take with you? I can go shopping for you after I go to the bank."

She shook her head, visibly retreating from him. It was probably for the best, for both of them, was his last thought before he dozed off.

He woke up a few hours later and immediately panicked when he realized Julie's side of the bed was empty. The shower wasn't running, and the house was scary quiet. He threw back the sheets, his heart thumping hard in his chest as he slipped and slid down the hall. Clyde, who was sitting on the counter, drinking from his water dish, stared at him, a very catlike what-the-fuck look on his face, before he leaped to the ground and exited the back door.

Julie must have left it open.

Wynn took a couple of deep breaths to settle his heart down and followed. The deck was wet, where she'd apparently rinsed it off, and she'd dragged one of the lounge chairs he kept around for Dani into the yard. The grass was soft under his bare feet as he crossed to where she was all stretched out, apparently sleeping.

"Have a good nap?" Her lips twisted into a gentle smile; her eyes were still closed.

"Yeah. How about you? Get any rest?" He knelt down beside her, relieved to see that she was fine even if she did look like she'd been crying.

"A little."

"I'll get dinner started." He leaned in, pressing a kiss to her temple, and headed for the kitchen.

Clyde had found a dry spot on the deck and was sunning himself, content in a way that Wynn envied as he stepped into the kitchen and took some chicken out of the freezer.

Cooking, especially for Julie, soothed him, and he found temporary comfort in dicing and slicing, opening cans and smoothing garlic butter on bread. He even found a bottle of Yellow Tail Chardonnay in the wine rack.

He'd just put it in the refrigerator to chill when Julie came back in. "I'm going to take a shower."

"Want some company?" They had at least thirty minutes until the tetrazzini was done.

"Sure."

Wynn checked the counters to make sure he'd left nothing out the cat would get into and followed her to his bedroom. "I'm glad John's gone."

"Why do you think I suggested he take the chip to your dad?" She grinned, laughing softly as she peeled her shirt over her head.

He reached out to help her, tossing her shirt aside and pushing her pants off her hips while her fingers worked at his clothes. Then his mouth was on hers; he sucked at her lips, drawing them up and kissing her, enjoying the feel of her soft curves pressed against the length of him.

"You still want that shower?" she asked, her lips pressed against his chest, her breath drifting across his skin.

"Do you?" He ran his fingers through her hair, pulling out the scrunchie that held it up on her head, combing the thick mass out with his fingers before burying his nose in it.

"I want one more go at that shower before I leave." Grinning, she took him by the hand and dragged him to the stall, flipping the lever as she went.

Wynn closed the door, and the glass immediately steamed up. So did things between them, neither of them bothering with soap as they touched each other.

He knelt between her legs, and she pushed her hips toward him as he parted the lips of her pussy, exposing her clit. Water ran down her abdomen, streaming perilously close to her already swollen clit before changing its path and sliding across his fingers to the tile below.

He leaned in and pulled it between his lips, enjoying the swell of tender flesh in his mouth as he caressed it, swirling his tongue around it. Her fingers tangled in his wet hair, Julie rode his tongue faster and faster until her cries bounced off the tile and glass.

She pushed him away, sagging against the shower wall, a satisfied smile on her face. "Fuck me."

She said it so softly, he almost didn't hear her above the shower jets. Happy to fulfill her request, he stood up, hoisting one of her legs over his arm. He guided his aching cock into her warm wetness, sighing at the intense wave of pleasure that rolled through him, but they were only halfway there. He grabbed her other leg, lifting it and pinning her to the shower wall. She moaned and tensed underneath him, her nails digging into his back while the shower beat a tattoo against his skin. They shifted slightly and she locked her legs around his waist.

"Comfy?"

"Very." She nodded for emphasis, her wet hair tickling his nose.

He began to piston his cock into her, reveling in the feel of her silky walls tightening on every thrust, his own need forcing him to cum much sooner than he'd planned. Finally, he sagged against her. Her lips warm and sweet against his neck, working their way upward and sucking at his earlobe.

"Don't worry, baby. You'll get your round two." He laughed, gently setting her down.

He silently washed every inch of her, neither of them feeling like they needed to waste words saying things that would get them nowhere. Or worse, saying things that could ruin their last night together.

They stopped again in the middle of dinner, then finished off the cold tetrazzini and the Chardonnay, cuddled up under a blanket in the backyard.

31

More than anything, I didn't want to take Wynn's money, but he'd insisted and he was right. I'd need it.

We cooked breakfast together, bacon and eggs, but both of us ended up just picking at our food. Clyde stood only a few feet away, munching on his kitty kibble, happily ignorant of the fact I was leaving.

"You really shouldn't let him do that."

"This isn't right." Wynn threw his fork down, letting it clatter against his plate.

"Yes, it is, Wynn. It's for the best, and we both know it." I'd packed last night, not that I actually had much packing to do, and my bags sat next to the back door.

"That doesn't mean I have to like it."

Wynn pulled to a stop at the doors leading to my gate. "Your ticket is at the counter under the name Bonnie James."

"Okay." I didn't know what else to say, or even where to look, and my throat was too thick with tears to work out long flowery speeches of thanks.

"You have your passport?"

"Yeah." I patted my purse where I'd stuck it earlier along with the iPod he'd pressed into my hand after breakfast. He'd loaded it with Portuguese lessons and some music he thought I'd like.

There was no sense making this the long, drawn-out good-bye I knew it could be. Sighing, I forced myself to grab the handle and open the door. "Take good care of Clyde for me."

"Take care of yourself," was the last thing I heard him say before I climbed out and slammed the door behind me.

The double doors swished open, and one more time, I girded myself to meet an unknown destiny.

Inside, I headed for the ticket counter, practically squealing with glee when I found out there was a layover in Miami. I briefly wondered if it had been deliberate on Wynn's part, but the attendant assured me most flights to São Paulo had the same layover.

So much for my plan to ditch Bonnie James and get a new ticket, in another city, for a flight to Miami as *Julie James*.

Walking through the airport to my gate, I stopped at a news-stand to check the *USA Today* headlines, even though I knew it was too soon for anything to show up in the press. Then again, if they couldn't find me to confirm the information I'd given them, they could very well dismiss me as a crackpot. Hopefully, the FDA wouldn't feel the same sense of trepidation.

Everything went off without a hitch, and the first thing I did when I got to Miami Beach was buy a prepaid cell phone number and call Lisa's friend, Candy.

"Candy, it's Julie. Have you heard from my sister recently?"

"How do I even know it's safe to tell you where Lisa is? She said you were in cahoots with some goon."

"I'm in Miami Beach, *alone,* and I kind of need to get lost, ya know?"

"Can I call you back at this number?"

"Sure."

The second thing I did was cut off my hair and dye it red. I was in the middle of admiring the new me in the hairstylist's mirror when my cell phone rang.

"Meet me at the Starbucks on Lincoln Road in thirty minutes, and if you're not alone, I'm walking away." She hung up before I could ask how I'd know her. I guess she'd just have to find me.

Turns out there were three, count them *three,* Starbucks on Lincoln, all within blocks of each other. And, of course, I found Candy at the third one I went to. Or rather, she found me.

I was standing in line, waiting to get a bottle of water and trying to discreetly figure out which of the assorted women might be Candy, when a tiny young woman slid into line behind me. She had gorgeous pale skin and blue (and not that pale, old-lady blue but an oh-my-God-look-at-her neon blue) hair. "Julie?"

"Yeah." I turned to look at her and just as quickly turned around when she snapped at me not to.

"Your family's in Puerto Rico."

Then I did look at her, with my jaw hanging on the ground. "Puerto Rico?"

She nodded, a silent confirmation, and disappeared into the thick afternoon crowd.

I blew out a heavy breath, wondering how in the hell I was going to find them once I got there.

EPILOGUE

Six Months Later

Hot and sweaty, I bent over to stretch my leg muscles and blew out a breath. Then I stood, stretching my arms over my head and admiring the sunset. I walked slowly, watching the tide creep up the beach and waiting for Karen to catch up.

Even though there was no Darcy to watch and no Tara to annoy me, I'd come to love Puerto Rico in the months I'd been here, and I'd even gotten fairly fluent in Spanish. It was about as far as you could get from the deserts of Arizona and West Texas, but jogging on the beach in February with temperatures hovering at a balmy seventy-five degrees was absolute heaven.

We'd settled in Luquillo, just outside of San Juan. Karen and Kevin leased a condo within walking distance of the place I shared with Lisa. She'd immersed herself in San Juan's nightlife, like the old pro party girl that she was. Karen and I just rolled our eyes, happy all three of us were together and safe and content to live at a much slower, much quieter pace.

I'd had enough excitement with Wynn and John to last me a

lifetime, but that didn't stop me from occasionally looking over my shoulder or keep the hairs on my neck from standing on end for no apparent reason. I didn't doubt that if Sunset could find us, they'd put bullets in all of us, but they were too busy fending off an investigation from the FDA, not to mention the lawsuits—lots of them. Kevin said they'd be tied up for years and way too busy to worry about us.

Thank God for small favors. If anyone came after me, it wouldn't be Wynn. I reached up to rub away the slight ache in the vicinity of my heart.

"You're thinking about him again," Karen said.

I snapped back to the present just in time to stumble in the sand. "So what's your point?" I panted.

"I just wish things could have worked out differently for you two is all."

"Maybe in the next lifetime." I gave her a smile that seemed to make my whole face tighten with the effort. "Come on. We better get you home before Kevin comes looking for us."

The condo was dark when I got home, a sure sign that Lisa was either at work, as a bartender, or out partying. And despite many requests to leave a light on when she left, the entire place was dark.

I dropped my keys on the entry hall table and flicked a switch, groaning when nothing happened. I tried again in the living room, flicking the wall switch, but no light came on. I'd begged Lisa to leave the damn blinds shut when she left, but she didn't do that either. I couldn't bitch too much, though, since the full moon shone through the sliding glass door, allowing me to see where I was going as I headed to my bedroom. I was ready for a hot shower and a glass of wine.

The bedroom light didn't work either, and I was beginning

to get concerned. I knew the lights in the building were on. I'd seen them coming in.

Being the oldest, I'd called dibs on the ocean view and also had a sliding glass door. Moonlight spilled across the bed, illuminating a ribbon-wrapped eight-by-ten box sitting near the end. My hands shook, and my legs turned to jelly as I scanned the bedroom, staring extra hard at the darkened corners for any shape resembling a man. Peering at the door to my walk-in closet and debating if it looked like it had when I went for my run. Glancing into the bathroom and meeting only my own startled expression in the mirror. Listening extra hard for the sound of someone else breathing. Checking over my shoulder to see if someone was in the living room.

Nothing, no one, nowhere.

As I crossed the bedroom and picked up the box, I didn't for a minute think Lisa'd gone shopping for me. Shaking the box made me wish I hadn't as an image of me scattered all over Luquillo filled my head.

Whatever it was rattled slightly, and I gave in to temptation, slowly tugging at the ribbon and tossing it aside. Blood beat a pulse in my ears, but that didn't stop me from lifting the lid and folding back the tissue. Inside was a silver framed photo of Clyde, wearing what looked to be a diamond collar no less.

"Hmmpf." I smiled to myself, thinking he looked fat and happy . . . and did I mention fat?

"What do you think?"

I shrieked and spun around, the photo flying through the air and landing a few feet away on the carpet. "Goddamnitall, Wynn!"

The sound of his laughter filled my ears as he flicked on the bathroom light. "Scare ya?"

"Fuck yeah!" I took a step toward him, ready to throw myself at him, then stopped, shuffling backward as excitement was replaced with fear. "Why are you here?"

"For you?"

My fists tightened, my nails biting into tender flesh of the palms of my hands. "You mean for your dad?"

"I told you, honey, I'm a lover not a fighter." His lips twitched and he started laughing again. "He wasn't too happy with you, but I made him see the light, with a little help from Mom."

"What light?"

"As Mom pointed out, you are a very clever young lady. You followed his demands, and our agreement, to the letter. The chip for your freedom."

The jangle of nerves in my belly still hadn't completely subsided, though. "And?"

"And"—he slowly began to move toward me—"I convinced him you'd be a hell of an asset to the family business."

Now my lips were twitching as I sank down on the bed. "An asset, huh?"

He pushed me back on the chenille bedspread, straddling my hips and lifting my shirt over my head. "Well, that and he can't very well put out a hit on his future daughter-in-law, now, can he?"

Turn the page
for a taste of "Hot Pepper,"
by P.F. Kozak!

In TRIO,
on sale now from Aphrodisia!

1

Pepper grabbed her purse and went out the back door, slamming it shut behind her. Her sister had really crossed the line this time. If it wasn't bad enough that she had to come crawling back home and ask for help, Lois wouldn't let her forget how she had disappointed everyone by leaving. This time, she had actually called her a failure, to her face.

She got into her car, which she hoped would start. It needed work. But that took money, which she didn't have. Damned if she would ask her sister for it. She would walk first.

When the motor turned over and started to hum, Pepper breathed a sigh of relief. She didn't know where the hell she would go, but she did know she wouldn't spend another night sleeping on her sister's couch.

Almost out of habit, she headed downtown. Maybe she would run into someone she knew. She smacked the steering wheel with her hand. And what if she did? What would she say?

"Oh, and by the way, can I sleep on your couch until I can afford my own place?"

Yeah, right.

She drove around for about half an hour, checking out some of her old haunts. The high school looked the same on the outside. Not having been in it for over ten years, she didn't know if she would recognize anything inside. The public library had already closed for the day, or she would have stopped to check her e-mail.

A new mall had opened on the edge of town. She didn't bother stopping there, either, since what little money she had needed to stay in her wallet. Then she drove down Elm Street and saw the sign for Buck's Bar and Grill. Lois told her only a few nights before that Ted owned the place now, since his father had passed away. She smiled, knowing she might have just found another sofa.

Pepper parked in the gravel parking lot between two pickup trucks. Obviously, some things never change. Buck's had always been popular with the after-work crowd, the guys stopping for a beer before going home. Later, anyone looking for some company for the evening would drop by, or couples would come in for a drink.

Everything inside looked the same as she remembered, except for the addition of white Christmas lights strung across the room and the pictures. Paintings she recognized as Ted's hung over the bar, as well as on the walls by the tables. She knew his father would never have allowed the lights, or his artwork, in here. Evidently, Ted really did run the place now.

Lois told her Ted would sometimes tend bar in the evenings, but the guy behind the bar tonight wasn't Ted. She didn't recognize him. Making her way past the men in work clothes and baseball caps, she managed to squeeze in at the end of the bar.

"Excuse me, is Ted here, please?"

The bartender gave her the once-over before he answered. "Yeah, he's in the office. What's your name?"

"Could you tell him Pepper would like to speak to him?"

"Sure will, sweetheart."

He disappeared through a side door for a few minutes. When he came back, Ted followed.

"Pepper? What the hell are you doing here? I thought you were still in Pittsburgh."

"Not anymore. I got laid off and ran out of money. I'm staying with my sister right now."

"Hey, kid. I'm sorry to hear that. Run over there and grab that table in the corner. I'll buy you a beer." Ted went behind the bar. He grabbed two bottles of Iron City and two glasses, and then came back to the table.

"Thanks, Ted. I can use a beer."

"Tell me what happened. I thought you were doing okay in Pittsburgh."

"I was. When my bank offered me the transfer to their headquarters, you know I jumped at it. I had no reason to stay here. I did okay, too. I learned the ropes. They made me a loan officer and sent me to school."

"Lois told me you got a promotion. I didn't know they made you an officer."

"Yeah, well, big effing deal. I got promoted and went to school. My last review was a good one. My supervisor told me I'd probably get promoted again within the next year. Then a bigger bank swallowed us up. They handed me my pink slip and told me not to let the door hit me in the ass. So much for making a better life for myself."

"You couldn't find anything else?"

"No. It's really bad right now. There aren't many jobs to be had, anywhere."

"What are you going to do?"

"Don't know." Pepper poured the rest of her beer into her glass. Screwing up her courage, she plunged in. "I have a favor to ask, actually maybe a couple of favors."

"Tell me what."

"I need a job and a place to stay for a while. I don't suppose you could use a waitress here and maybe have a sofa I can sleep on?" Pepper raised her glass and took a sip. Her hand shook a little. She hoped Ted hadn't noticed.

"What about your sister? She doesn't have room for you?"

"I'm sleeping on her sofa, have been for almost a week. Every day, I hear the lecture of how I should have been a beautician like her. Today, she told me if I weren't so stuck up, I wouldn't be such a failure."

"She said that to you?"

"She sure as hell did. That's when I left and came here. I drove around awhile, and ended up on your doorstep."

"Jesus Christ, Pepper. You'd think after all this time, she would have softened a little."

"Not a chance. You know, once a bitch, always a bitch. I had noplace else to go. I thought I could put up with it until I could find a job and save enough for my own place. But, after today, I'd rather sleep in my car than hear her mouth off to me again."

Ted flagged the bartender to bring them two more beers. "If you want a job here, it's yours. As you can see, business is good. You could fill in on the floor when I need extra help, but I think it would make more sense if you help me with the books. With your banking experience, you'll probably handle the accounting better than I ever could."

"God, thank you, Ted. You've always been a good friend."

Ted nervously tapped his fingers on the table. Pepper remembered he always did that when he felt uncomfortable. He confirmed her suspicion when he said, "We have to talk about the other."

The disappointment welled up in her throat. She tried to swallow it. "It's all right. I understand I can't intrude on your life."

"Pepper, it's not that, not at all. This is more about you than about me."

"I don't understand."

"Butch is staying with me right now, has been for several months."

"He is? What about Sandy?"

"They finally called it quits. Sandy agreed to a no-fault divorce if Butch gave her custody of Stacy. It's over."

"Lois didn't tell me."

"Probably because everyone sides with Sandy. Butch left her."

"Why? I know he loves their kid."

"Yes, but he doesn't love Sandy. He never has."

"He should have thought of that before he knocked her up." She took a good swig of Iron City.

"You're still pissed at him, aren't you?"

"Why the hell shouldn't I be? He fucked up both our lives by getting her pregnant. You know damn well I thought we'd get married."

"Yes, and I also know he still talks about you."

"He does? How do you know that?"

"I live with him, remember?"

"Yeah, you told me that. Shit, if I stay with you, I'll be living with him, too!"

"That's my point. I have the space. My dad left me everything. That big old house is all mine. When Butch asked me if I'd rent him a room, I thought, what the hell, why not?"

"That's how he ended up with you?"

"You know my house is close to his garage. That's good for him, and I like having the company. Can you handle living in the same house with him?"

"Ted, I don't have many options right now. If you have a place for me to sleep, and a shower I can use, I'll deal with it."

"Well, in all fairness, I can't offer that to you until I talk to Butch. He has dibs."

"Yeah, I remember. Dibs is sacred."

"You know, he still does that. He'll call dibs on a piece of cold pizza in the damn refrigerator." Ted took his cell phone out of his pocket. "Let me call him. If he's home, it'll only take him a few minutes to get here."

While Ted called Butch, Pepper went to the ladies' room. She put on some lipstick and checked her hair. She hadn't seen Butch since she left Willows Point. The last time she saw him, he'd come into the bank to make a deposit. He'd heard she planned to move to Pittsburgh, and asked if she wanted to have a good-bye drink with him. She said no. There had been no contact between them since.

When she came back, she saw Ted behind the bar talking to the bartender. She waited for him at their table. He came back carrying another bottle of Iron City and a glass. "I got him. He'll be here in about ten minutes."

"Did you tell him I'm here?"

"I told him you're back in Willows Point. I didn't say anything about your moving in with us." Ted grabbed another chair from the next table and put it between them. "I figure we'll ask him together. Let him say no to your face. I bet he can't."

Pepper pressed her cool glass against her cheek. Her face felt hot. "Ted, before he gets here, I want to know for sure that you're all right with this. I don't know if you're involved with anyone. Will my being around be a problem?"

"I'm not involved with anyone, and your being around won't be a problem."

"What happened to John?"

"It didn't work out. We went different directions."

"When Lois told me you moved back home, I wondered what happened."

"The next promising art student came along and that, as they say, was that."

"I'm sorry, Ted. I didn't know. God, I really didn't mean to lose track of you guys. It just happened."

"This feels like no time has passed since I saw you last." Ted put his hand over hers. "You know, Pepper, Butch isn't the only one who thought of you over the years. I still remember our wild days."

"So do I." Pepper squeezed his hand. "The three of us really had something special in high school. You were the only one who really understood when Butch dumped me."

"He didn't want to. With his parents and Sandy's family pressuring him to do the right thing . . . he caved. He married her because he had to, not because he wanted to."

"Yeah, right. That, and my E-Z Pass, will get me on the turnpike."

"Look, Pepper, I know he hurt you. I also know one of the reasons you took the job in Pittsburgh was to get away from him. But that's water under the bridge now. You're right. We did have something special together. That's why I think it could work if you moved in with us."

"Do you mind if I ask you something?"

"What?"

"Have you and Butch done anything together since he's moved in?"

"Absolutely nothing."

Pepper scratched Ted's wrist with her fingernails. "So, you've both become monks?"

"More or less."

"That really sucks."

"As I recall, so do you, very well."

"Okay, I'll pay my share of the rent with blow jobs. Is that the deal?"

Ted smiled. "It could work. There aren't many women that can give me a hard-on. You're one of the very few. In fact, you're giving me one now. There's something to be said for that."

Pepper glanced at the locals sitting at the bar. "Do they know you swing both ways?"

"Not really. If I make jokes about big tits a few times a week, they're all satisfied I'm one of them."

"Even with your painting?"

Ted pointed to the far end of the bar. "See that guy down there, the one with the Pirates ball cap?"

"Yeah, what about him?"

"He bought one of my landscapes for his wife's birthday. Says she really likes what I do and surprised her with it."

"No kidding!"

"No kidding. Because I went to school there, I also got an exhibit at Indiana University. I sold about half a dozen from that show, flowers and landscapes mostly. I've even sold a few right here." He gestured to the wall behind them. "All these are for sale, except for that one."

Pepper looked at the painting that wasn't for sale. "Is that the field where you, me, and Butch had our picnics?"

"Same one. That's why it isn't for sale." A few moments of uncomfortable silence followed, as Pepper struggled with the memory. Ted kept the conversation going. "Yeah, between painting and the bar, I've been busy."

Pepper tried her best to keep things light. "Glad things are good for you. How's Butch doing?"

"Butch is doing okay, too, even with the divorce. He's running the garage now. His uncle retired."

"Think he'll fix my car for a blow job?"

"Why don't you ask him? He just came in the door."

Pepper looked toward the door. Butch hadn't yet seen them sitting in the corner. He had his head turned, looking for them at the bar. Her heart thumped in her chest as she stared at his profile. His Roman nose and curly black hair were just as she remembered. He had a suntan, making his olive skin even darker. In his jeans and T-shirt, he still looked every bit the hot Italian stud.

She jumped when Ted put his hand on her arm. "Steady, Pepper, you're shaking."

"Shit!" She took a deep breath and shook her hands, hoping to dry her sweating palms. "Ted, I might need something stronger than a beer."

"You got it, kiddo. I'll get us a bottle." Before going behind the bar, he stopped and spoke to Butch. Pepper saw Ted point back to the corner table and Butch nodded. When Butch turned and came toward her, she put her hands in her lap so he wouldn't see them shaking.

"Hello, Pepper. It's been a long time." He bent over and kissed her cheek.

"Hi, Butch. You're looking good."

"So are you." Butch sat down in the chair next to her. "How've you been?"

"Not too bad. And you?"

"I'm doing all right."

Fortunately, Ted returned at that moment and interrupted the banal conversation. He put a bottle of Jim Beam and three shot glasses on the table. He glanced at Pepper. "Everything okay here?"

"Fine." Pepper hoped that sounded believable. "Could you pour me a shot?"

Butch picked up an empty shot glass. "Me, too."

"Shots all around." Ted opened the bottle of whiskey and poured them each a drink. Pepper concentrated on keeping her hand still and picked up her glass. Ted picked up his and raised it to his companions. "To friends reunited."

Butch raised his and toasted in Italian. *"Cin Cin."*

Pepper offered a weak "Cheers," and then bolted back her shot. She held out her glass for a refill.

Ted poured another one. "Have you had any dinner, Pepper? You don't want this to knock you on your ass."

"No, I haven't eaten anything. I left before Lois finished cooking dinner."

"You'd better eat something, so you don't get shitfaced." Ted flagged down the waitress. "Butch, you want a burger?"

"Sure, and a side of your greasy fries, too."

"Fuck you! You're not paying, so quit complaining."

"Well, hell, if it's on the house, throw in an order of wings, too." His typical Butch wisecrack didn't hide his concern. "What the hell happened, Pepper? Why aren't you in Pittsburgh?"

The urge to cry nearly overcame Pepper. She drank her second shot before she answered. "I lost my job." That's all she could say. The waitress came just then to take their order, giving her a chance to get it together.

After Ted ordered them some food, he told Butch what Pepper had told him, sparing her the ordeal of having to tell her story again. While Butch listened, he focused on Ted, but held Pepper's hand. The familiar feel of his fingers wrapped around hers calmed her. Ted stopped just short of asking Butch about her staying with them.

Ted picked up the bottle and poured Pepper another shot. "I'll let Pepper ask you what she asked me."

"Ask me what?"

With Butch still holding her hand, and with his dark eyes fixed solely on her, Pepper plunged in. "I asked Ted if I can stay with him for awhile, until I get on my feet. He's already said I can work here at the bar, but told me you have dibs on the house."

"You know about me and Sandy? We got divorced?"

"Ted just told me. I didn't know when I asked to stay with him, and I didn't know you had moved in with him."

"What the fuck difference does that make?" Butch turned to Ted. "You got a problem with her staying in your house if I'm there?"

"Not at all. But I thought you might."

"Why?" Butch never had been one to pull any punches. His shoot-from-the-hip style had survived his failed marriage. "Do you think Sandy put me off women?"

"If she had, at least I'd be getting some. We both know that's not the case."

"Then, why do you think I'd have a problem with Pepper staying with us?"

"If you're asking me that, I guess there isn't one. If you both can handle it, then let's try it. Who knows? It just might work."

Butch squeezed Pepper's hand. "Do you think you can handle it, Pearl?"

"Don't you start that already! You know I hate that name. My name is Pepper."

"You can't bullshit me, Pearl. I know that's your real name. Your mama told my mama she named you after Minnie Pearl. I remember when your grandmother gave you a straw hat with flowers and a price tag hanging from it on your sixteenth birthday."

"Fuck you!"

"I also remember that." He tilted his head toward Ted. "I think that's what Rembrandt here is talking about. We have history, Pepper. Can you live with that every day?"

Pepper stuck her chin out defiantly. "I can if you can, Robert."

Ted interrupted. "All right, boys and girls. Play nice."

Butch shot Ted a look that curled Pepper's toes. "You mean the way we used to play?"

"Maybe." He grinned at Pepper. "Chances are good you'll get your car fixed."

"What's her car got to do with it?"

"Her car needs work. Just before you came in, she mentioned asking you if she could arrange a barter. Tell him, Pepper."

"Ted, for Christ's sake!"

"Pepper, what the hell is he talking about? What kind of barter?"

"Since I don't have enough money to get my car fixed, I wondered if you'd work on it for a blow job. It was a joke, for crying out loud!"

Ted laughed. "She also might end up paying me rent the same way. What do you think?"

"I think life just got a whole hell of a lot better!"

Pepper drank her third shot and held up her shot glass. "I want another one."

Ted put the cap back on the bottle. "Not until you eat something." He set the bottle on the floor beside his chair. "I don't want to have to carry you out of here."

"Party pooper."

"If you do move in with us, kiddo, the party is just starting."

"That's the goddamn truth." Butch opened the extra beer and drank it out of the bottle. "Do you have your stuff in your car?"

"No. All I have with me is my purse. Everything else is still at Lois's house."

"How bad was it when you left? Can you go back tonight and get your clothes?"

"I think so. Maybe I'll be lucky and she'll just ignore me."

"I'll go with you."

Ted tapped his fingers on the table. "Butch, I don't think that's a good idea. I'll go."

"Why the hell shouldn't I go? I don't give a shit what Lois thinks of me. My life is none of her goddamned business."

226

"Lois is already being a bitch to Pepper. If you show up, it'll be even worse."

Pepper agreed. "Butch, Ted's right. Let him help me get my stuff. There's not that much. I sold all my furniture so I could fit everything in my car. Other than my clothes, I only brought back my TV, my stereo, my laptop, and a few boxes of things. Most of it is still packed. I've been living out of my suitcase."

"Damn it, Pepper, it should be me."

"That's what I said ten years ago."

Butch reached into his back pocket and took out his wallet. "Let me show you something." He flipped through his credit cards until he came to the last sleeve. He carefully pulled out a picture he had tucked behind the card and handed it to Pepper.

Pepper stared at an image of herself in a white sundress, her long reddish brown hair framing her face. She remembered the day Ted took the picture. The three of them had gone on a pic-nic the day after they graduated, in the same field Ted had painted. Ted took his camera. He decided he wanted to paint her in the white sundress. She had posed for him, so he would have the shots to work from. Butch asked him for a copy of his favorite.

"You kept this?"

"Of course I did."

"Why?"

Butch shifted in his chair, then took a sip of beer. "You were beautiful that day." He stared at her for a moment. "You still are."

Pepper's eyes filled with tears. "This was the last time . . ." She couldn't continue.

Butch finished her thought. "It was the last time the three of us were together. I found out a week later that Sandy was preg-nant, and all hell broke loose."

Pepper squeezed her eyes shut, trying to keep the tears in-side. She remembered being with Butch and Ted that day. They had made sure they went to an isolated spot, where no one would see them. She hadn't worn anything under the sundress. Ted had asked her not to, so she would surprise Butch. The three of them made love on a blanket, surrounded by daisies. It was the happiest day of her life.

She hadn't been with either of them since.